D0034824

THE LUCKY ONES

THE LUCKY ONES

LINDA WILLIAMS JACKSON

CANDLEWICK PRESS

First edition 2022

Library of Congress Catalog Card Number 2021947068
ISBN 978-1-5362-2255-5

22 23 24 25 26 27 LBM 10 9 8 7 6 5 4 3 2 1

Printed in Melrose Park, IL, USA

This book was typeset in Fairfield LH.

Candlewick Press
99 Dover Street
Somerville, Massachusetts 02144

www.candlewick.com

This book is dedicated to all my siblings,
especially Willie Mae and Odell,
whom we lost to COVID-19 in 2020.

Wilsonville, Mississippi

1967

FRIDAY, MARCH 17

A Whole Moon Pie to Myself

"THANK YOU, MR. FOSTER!"

Ellis Earl Brown waved goodbye to his teacher, then trekked with his sister Carrie Ann along the dusty path toward home. Mr. Julius Foster always offered to drive his lime-green station wagon all the way to the end of the winding path to drop Ellis Earl and Carrie Ann off directly in front of their house. But regardless of how much eight-year-old Carrie Ann begged him to accept the ride, eleven-year-old Ellis Earl *always* adamantly refused, even when the sky threatened rain, as it did today. Ellis

Earl was grateful that Mr. Foster was kind enough to include them in his carpool of nine students to whom he gave a ride to and from school each day, but Ellis Earl didn't want the other students to see the place they called home.

Because it was Friday, Carrie Ann began skipping down the road singing a made-up song about how glad she was that she didn't have to get up for school the next morning. But Ellis Earl dreaded the weekend. The weekend meant two whole days with no school and no grand selection of books from Mr. Foster's shelf, except the one book Ellis Earl was allowed to take home to read to his younger siblings and the one book he was allowed to take for himself.

Today he wasn't at all happy with his selection. Ellis Earl preferred the books with lots of pictures. But his friend Philip loved the Hardy Boys mysteries, and this is what he had challenged Ellis Earl to take home for the weekend. Ellis Earl wasn't interested in reading *The Secret of the Old Mill*. But not wanting to be called a chicken, he had accepted the challenge and brought the book home. For certain, he'd do his best to try to read it, as he longed to read chapter books like Philip. But deep down he knew that his mind would soon wander away from the words if there were no pictures to guide him along.

Besides the absence of Mr. Foster's collection of books, there would also be the absence of food—sometimes not even a piece of bread—unless Ellis Earl's family went to visit their grandparents on Sunday, which he dreaded.

This weekend, however, Ellis Earl was in luck. Mr. Foster had given him the leftovers from a surprise afternoon snack for his class. Ellis Earl wished the food could hold them over until Monday. But with eleven people in their house, a half loaf of bread, a half-empty jar of peanut butter, two chocolate Moon Pies, and a package of Stage Planks wouldn't last until even the next day. The minute Mr. Foster had given him the sack, Ellis Earl had begun figuring out how many sandwiches he could make with the bread and peanut butter. He shared those figures with Carrie Ann.

"We got ten slices of bread," he said. "We can make five sandwiches and cut 'em in half, or we can each have one slice with peanut butter on top. That's enough for all the children. We'll divide up the Moon Pies, too. Mama can have the Stage

Planks. It'll be nice if she has something sweet for a change."

Carrie Ann stopped skipping and turned to face Ellis Earl. She glared at him. "Mr. Foster said to make sho' I got a Moon Pie," she said. "That mean a *whole* Moon Pie. So I ain't splittin' it up with nobody."

Ellis Earl waved her off. "Don't be selfish. We can split these Moon Pies six ways. Everybody oughta get to taste something sweet."

"I'm hungry enough to eat both of them Moon Pies *and* all that bread and peanut butter right now," Carrie Ann said, licking her lips.

"Stop acting greedy. We can't eat up everything by ourselves. It ain't right."

Having eaten only one meal that day himself, Ellis Earl would have gladly eaten all the food right then and there had he been as oblivious to their family's plight as his younger sister was. But he wasn't as oblivious as Carrie Ann, so he would never think of devouring a whole sack of food and not sharing it with his siblings, especially ten-year-old Oscar, who had become too ill to attend school.

Ellis Earl knew that all the family who were home during the day had probably eaten little more than a couple of biscuits, at best. He was fortunate that Mr. Foster always brought lunch for his students. Mr. Foster's food was delicious, so Ellis Earl didn't mind one bit that he couldn't bring his own lunch. Sometimes Mr. Foster even had fried chicken, or smothered pork chops. And as if by some trick of magic, he had enough for everyone, even the students who brought their own lunches at times.

"Why we gotta walk all the way home from the road?" Carrie Ann complained as she did nearly every day. She hugged her stack of textbooks to her chest with one hand and with the other tugged her coat collar tighter about her neck. "It's cold out here. And my hand is freezing."

Ellis Earl clucked his tongue at Carrie Ann. It was a pity how his little sister could so quickly switch from skipping and singing to slouching and complaining. He peered through the still-bare branches of the trees and gazed at the sky. It was overcast and gray. "It's about to be springtime before long," he said, even though he hardly believed that himself. Regretfully, he didn't have a free hand with which to secure his coat collar tighter about his neck. Neither could he alternate which hand held his textbooks in order to warm the other in his coat pocket as Carrie Ann did. But cold hands were a small price to pay to avoid the humiliation he would feel if the other children in the carpool ever saw his house.

"When?" Carrie Ann asked.

"When what?"

"When is spring gon' be here?"

Ellis Earl shrugged. "Couple of weeks, I think."

"What *day*?"

"How should I know? Do I look like a calendar?"

"You always lookin' at it, so I thought you had it re-memorized by now."

"Well, I don't have it *memorized*. I just know spring's coming soon. But I don't know the exact day." Ellis Earl glanced back up at the sky, doubtful. Spring was nowhere in sight, despite what the calendar said. But oh, how he wished it were. March shouldn't feel the same as December.

Another cold night in their house.

Another night that his brother Oscar would be coughing up a storm.

Ellis Earl hoped that Oscar would get better soon. He had missed two months of school, but Ellis Earl knew he could catch up if he was able to go back before the term was over. Oscar was a fast learner. But in the meantime, Oscar would have to settle for the bits of the outside world that Ellis Earl could bring, like books and food, when Mr. Foster sent it home with him.

Halfway to the house, Carrie Ann stopped and stamped her foot.

Ellis Earl groaned. "Now what's the matter?"

"*Please* let me have something outta that sack 'foe we get to the house," Carrie Ann begged.

"Nope. This food is for everybody."

Carrie Ann dropped her books on the road, fell to her knees, and, with her hands clasped beneath her chin, begged. "Please! Just gimme my Moon Pie. I just wanna have a whole Moon Pie to myself for once. Just. This. One. Time. *Please!*"

Ellis Earl's shoulders drooped. Carrie Ann was right. When they were lucky enough to have a sweet treat, it was always "divided up" among the little children: him, Oscar, Carrie Ann, Beatrice, Deidra, and Vera. Regardless of how tiny the snack, whether it was a Moon Pie, a Honey Bun, or even a Poor Boy cake, it was divided up.

While Ellis Earl was deciding what to do, Carrie Ann got to her feet and reminded him again, "Mr.

Foster said to make sho' I got a Moon Pie. That mean a *whole* Moon Pie. Not no split-up Moon Pie."

"Mr. Foster said to make *sure* you got a Moon Pie, not *sho'*."

"Well, if that ain't the pot callin' the kettle black," said Carrie Ann. "Don't try to tell me how to talk, Ellis Earl Brown. You ain't always so proper yo'self."

"*Your*self," said Ellis Earl, unfazed.

Carrie Ann stretched out her hand. "Just gimme my Moon Pie."

With much exaggeration, Ellis Earl placed his books on the road, reached into the bag, and pulled out a Moon Pie. "Here," he said, extending it toward Carrie Ann.

"Thank the good Lord!" cried Carrie Ann.

Before they reached the house, she had devoured the whole Moon Pie. With a satisfied grin, she raced toward the rickety steps of their home, dashed up, and darted across the porch to the front door.

Ellis Earl, however, hesitated at the edge of the yard. With his stomach rumbling, he peeked into the sack and considered eating that entire second Moon Pie.

But he thought of Oscar.

He thought of Beatrice.

He thought of Deidra.

He thought of Vera.

Split four ways, that Moon Pie would make a satisfying treat for them.

He himself could do without.

Four Extra Mouths

Trudging toward the front steps, Ellis Earl stared glumly at the weatherworn shack sitting atop large cinder blocks. The walls of its three equal-size rooms, straight in a row, seemed barely strong enough to hold up the rusted tin roof that covered them. Ellis Earl hated how the house rattled when strong winds blew. Oh, how he wished his family lived in one of those sturdy brick houses he'd seen in town!

To himself, he whispered this mantra: "One day I *will* live in a sturdy brick house."

In the meantime, one thing he could be grateful

for as the steps, then the porch, creaked beneath his feet was the smoke rising from the chimney. That meant they still had enough wood for the heater, and the house wouldn't be too cold for the night. And maybe Oscar wouldn't be coughing all night.

All the same, he gazed up at the sky, begging it to bind up winter and send down spring. Instead the gray sky mocked him with a drop of rain that, within seconds, turned into a chilly drizzle. Ellis Earl hurried toward the front door. It was enough that Oscar was sick; Mama didn't need two children to fret over through the night.

The moment Ellis Earl entered the front door and smelled beans and the beckoning aroma of cornbread, a bubble of joy floated to his heart.

Given that the day before, the only food in the kitchen had been just enough flour, lard, and milk to make biscuits for the day, the scent of beans and cornbread meant their uncle Joseph had stopped by. No doubt after seeing the near-empty food safe and icebox, he had gone out and purchased a bag of beans, rice, cornmeal, sugar, and milk—enough food to get Ellis Earl's family through a few days at least.

Ellis Earl smiled. He was happy he hadn't eaten the extra Moon Pie after all. He wanted to be selfless like his uncle Joseph.

Ellis Earl was barely inside the front door before his three-year-old niece practically tackled him. Vera always hugged him when he arrived home, but today's greeting was especially enthusiastic. Ellis Earl knew that Vera was happy to see him. But he also knew that Vera was equally happy to see the brown paper sack. And more importantly, Vera knew that, tucked between Ellis Earl's textbooks, there was the storybook that he was allowed to borrow from Mr. Foster's collection.

Vera slipped the book from the stack and beamed. "*Curious George Rides a Bike*!" She hugged the book to her chest. She knew both the title and most of the text by heart. Next Vera reached for the sack, but Ellis Earl refused her. "You gotta wait like everybody else. Besides, we got beans today. We can save this for tomorrow."

With a nod, Vera scampered back to the floor, where she had been playing with dolls made from cardboard. For a moment, Ellis Earl watched his niece and two of his sisters, seven-year-old Beatrice and six-year-old Deidra, play. He was glad they at least had *something* to do during the day, though he wished they could go to school like Carrie Ann and him. But there was not enough space in Mr. Foster's station wagon for all the Brown children. Even Oscar, after having become ill in January, had lost his spot to a third-grade boy named Larry.

Ellis Earl often wondered what would happen when Oscar got better. Would Larry have to give up his spot? Or would Oscar simply have to stay home? He hoped that during the next school year, the county would provide the bus that they had been promising for two years. Then all the children could go to school.

It was only four in the afternoon, but Oscar was already in bed, or on his mattress rather, next to the wood-burning heater in the front room. Ellis Earl placed his books on a cinder block in the corner, then headed over to where Oscar lay. He knelt beside the mattress and touched his brother's forehead. It was warm.

He stroked his cheek and Oscar's eyes fluttered open. They looked as if all the life had been drained from them.

"How you feelin'?" asked Ellis Earl.

"Tired," Oscar answered. His voice was croaky,

as if he hadn't spoken in days. He mustered the strength to raise his head and clear his throat. "What you bring me today?" He had asked Ellis Earl this same question every day since he began missing school.

Ellis Earl smiled, opened the sack, and pulled out the bread. "Mr. Foster gave us some food."

At the sight of store-bought bread, Oscar's tired eyes attempted a dance. "Mr. Foster so nice," he said quietly. He lowered his head and allowed his eyes to drift shut again.

Ellis Earl leaned over and hugged him. "Get better soon," he said. "Don't want you sick on your birthday. We gotta celebrate us both being eleven at the same time."

Even though their older brothers, seventeen-year-old Aaron and Andre, were twins, it was Ellis Earl and Oscar who were often mistaken for such, because they were so close in age and were exactly the same height. Born only eleven months apart—Oscar in April and Ellis Earl in May—the boys were always excited when, for one month, they were the same age.

"I'm gonna get you something this year," said Ellis Earl.

With a tired grin and his eyes still closed, Oscar replied, "You say that every year."

"But I'm gonna try real hard this year," said Ellis Earl. "I'm gonna get you something. Just you watch."

Oscar opened his eyes and smiled at Ellis Earl. "Ah, you don't have to get me nothin'," he said. "Besides, I can't get you nothin' for yo' birthday. So we even."

"I'm still gonna try," said Ellis Earl.

Oscar closed his eyes again. "I know you is," he whispered.

Are, thought Ellis Earl, but out loud he said, "And I'm gonna make it real special, too, since you've been sick so long."

"Thanks, brother," said Oscar.

Before Ellis Earl could carry his sack to the kitchen, his ear was turned to the sound of a car pulling into the yard. Without looking, he knew it was his oldest brother, twenty-two-year-old Walter Jr., for Junior's car made a loud, clanking noise as soon as it was shifted into park.

Ellis Earl rushed to the window, pulled back the threadbare curtain, and pressed his face against the dull pane in order to see out. His brother's

1950 Chevrolet Deluxe four-door sedan, a car with ten times more dents than doors, was parked all the way up to the porch steps. Inside sat the entire family: Junior; his wife, Sylvia; and their children, four-year-old Jewel, three-year-old Pearline, two-year-old Lil' Walt, and one-year-old Prince. The Stair Steppers, as some folks called them, because, born one year after the other, they were stacked up like stairs.

All the same, Sylvia was having another baby. And she was due to deliver soon. The four little ones would be staying at Ellis Earl's house. This way, Junior would be prepared at a moment's notice to rush Sylvia (who was leery of having a midwife deliver her baby) to the hospital two towns over.

And since no one can predict the exact day a new baby will choose to arrive, no one could give an exact amount of time the four little ones would be staying. Ellis Earl's shoulders drooped at the thought.

His niece Vera lived with them, but that was because her mother, Ellis Earl's oldest sister, Eloise, was deceased. But just as he had the past three times his sister-in-law, Sylvia, had a baby, Ellis Earl had hoped she would ask someone in her own family to "watch the babies" while she "had the baby." There were already way too many people in their tiny house. They hardly had any place to sleep. He and Oscar slept in the front room on a mattress. Mama and the girls slept in the middle room, where six of them shared two beds. And the three teenage boys, twins Andre and Aaron and the third wheel, fifteen-year-old Raymond, slept on pallets in the kitchen.

And there was definitely never enough food to go around.

Now there would be four extra mouths to feed.

And eight extra hands expecting something from the sack.

With that thought, Ellis Earl *wished* he'd eaten that Moon Pie while he'd had the chance. There would be no point in dividing such a small treat among so many.

By the time his oldest brother and his family bounded up the steps (Sylvia waddled, actually) and onto the porch, fourteen-year-old Jeannette had made her way to the front room from the kitchen in the back of the house.

Jeannette was the official keeper of the house and the official watcher of the younger children while Mama, Andre, Aaron, and Raymond went out to find work each day. And though she was fourteen, Jeannette was not an inch taller than eleven-year-old Ellis Earl—if you didn't count the high Afro covering her head. But by her own assessment, she was ten times wiser.

"Junior 'n 'em here?" she asked gruffly.

Ellis Earl nodded.

"Hope they brought they own food. We ain't got enough food to feed all them children."

Ellis Earl held up his sack. "I got stuff to make peanut butter sandwiches. That'll help."

Jeannette snatched the sack from Ellis Earl and examined its contents. She grabbed the package of Stage Planks and stuck it in the pocket of her dress.

"Hey! I'm saving that for Mama," said Ellis Earl. "I'm gonna give it to her when she gets home from work."

Jeannette glared at him. "She ain't gon' miss what she never had." She shoved the sack back toward Ellis Earl. "We still ain't got enough food to last till Junior come back for these children since God only know when that'll be."

"At least we got beans," said Ellis Earl.

"And a house full of people," said Jeannette. "We be lucky to get five darn beans apiece."

"They're just little children, Jeannette," said Ellis Earl, feeling guilty for having only moments before thought the same way himself.

"Some greedy lil' children," said Jeannette. "You seen Jewel lately? How fast she growing? Looking 'bout six, and she ain't but four. And Prince? He ain't but one, and near 'bout big as Vera already. Them children gon' eat us outta house and home by the time Junior come pick 'em back up."

Ellis Earl thought about the empty food safe and icebox in the kitchen. Even with the food from Uncle Joseph and the sack from Mr. Foster, there wasn't much house and home to be eaten out of. But he didn't dare point that out to Jeannette.

With a slight knock and before an official invitation to enter, Sister-in-Law Sylvia—a petite woman with a belly like a giant beach ball—tottered into the house.

Jeannette gritted her teeth and headed back to the kitchen.

Ellis Earl's younger sisters and his niece Vera dashed to the door to embrace Sylvia. Unlike Ellis Earl and Jeannette, they were thrilled to see her, and even more thrilled to pat her poked-out belly and inquire about the baby.

Seeing that neither his brother nor his sister-in-law brought in a grocery sack, Ellis Earl quietly left the front room and carried *his* sack to the kitchen. Somehow, he would figure out how to spread what little he had among so many.

Times Is Hard for Everybody

ELLIS EARL'S STOMACH GROWLED loudly as he waited in line to be served. Lined up before him in order by age were Deidra, Beatrice, and Carrie Ann. The littlest ones—Jewel, Vera, Pearline, Prince, and Lil' Walt—already sat on the floor of the kitchen, eating their bowls of beans. Oscar's bowl awaited him if he felt like eating later.

During times of plenty—when the flour, the cornmeal, and the lard buckets were full, when there were enough bags of beans and rice in the safe to last for days, when there were enough beans in the pot that a rumbling stomach could expect second helpings, when a spoonful of sugar was spilled and no one yelled at the spiller—suppertime at the Brown household was a boisterous affair of laughter and creativity.

Though beans and cornbread were often the only items on the menu, Ellis Earl and his siblings found joy in dressing them up for a taste competition. One might wonder how a person could dress up a bowl of pinto beans, but the Brown children had learned to get quite creative with whatever else could be found in the icebox or the wooden food safe, such as home-canned pear, peach, and fig preserves, which they had received from Uncle Joseph. Sometimes they even had molasses or ketchup to mix in with their beans. Ellis Earl's favorite way to dress up his beans was to turn them into what he liked to call bean pudding—cornbread crumbled into the beans, and the combo creamed together with a dollop of ketchup and a heaping spoonful of sugar.

But tonight disappointment visited Ellis Earl, as the icebox was void of anything other than the buttermilk his uncle Joseph had bought.

Tonight was not a night of laughter and creativity.

Tonight was a night of lack.

Not being one to complain, Ellis Earl took his place at the table after Jeannette ladled out just enough beans to fill half his bowl. The cornbread, too, was cut smaller than usual.

But Carrie Ann, *being* one to complain, gave Jeannette an evil eye and asked, "How come you can't fill my bowl up all the way?"

Jeannette pointed at the nieces and nephews sitting on the floor. "Don't you see all these bellies these beans have to fill?"

Carrie Ann shrugged. "Them lil' children don't need that much."

"Well, that's all you gittin'," said Jeannette. "These beans gotta last till tomorrow. Now, go on to the table and eat."

"Humph," said Carrie Ann, stomping away. "Bet you gon' fill yo' bowl all the way up."

While the youngest of the Browns sat on the floor, the younger Browns—Ellis Earl, Carrie Ann, Beatrice, and Deidra—stood at the table because they had no chairs on which to sit. The older Browns—Andre and Aaron, Raymond, and Jeannette—ate their supper in the middle room, where they sat on the two beds where Mama and the girls slept. Besides two old rocking chairs in the front room, the beds were the only place in the house to sit.

Mama ate her meal alone in the front room, where she sometimes listened to her battery-powered radio given to her by Uncle Joseph. Usually her children respected her privacy, as this was her only respite from her daily duties of working, or trying to *find* work, and worrying. But on this night, Ellis Earl left his place at the table to join Mama in the front room, hoping she wouldn't mind his wanting to have his own respite from the crowd (and Carrie Ann's constant complaining) in the kitchen.

Ellis Earl hesitated in the doorway between the middle room and the front room. Mama had only recently gotten home from work. He knew how much she cherished this time to herself. Yet he wanted badly to be with her.

Except for the creaking of the rocking chair where Mama sat and the crackling of the fire in the wood-burning heater, the front room was silent. Mama's tired face glowed in the amber light of the kerosene lamp. She slowly raised a spoonful of beans to her mouth, so lost in thought she didn't notice Ellis Earl watching her.

Mama startled when Andre, the older of the

twins by a full twenty minutes, yelled from the middle room, "Boy, why is you standing there staring at Mama like you ain't got good sense? Go on in the front room if you goin'."

Worry lines crinkled Mama's forehead. "What's the matter, Earl?"

Embarrassed that his brother had yelled at him, Ellis Earl dropped his head and asked, "Can I sit in here with you?"

"'Course you can," Mama answered.

Ellis Earl trudged into the room and sat in the other rocking chair. It creaked loudly.

"Something wrong, baby?" Mama asked, whispering so she wouldn't wake Oscar, who was curled up on the mattress. Even without whispering, Mama's voice was always soft. Soft and tired-sounding.

Ellis Earl replied, "Ain't nothing wrong. I just wanna sit in here with you."

Mama smiled. "I'd like that."

Mama's smile brought tiny lines around her eyes. Ellis Earl wished he could erase them. He wasn't ready for wrinkles to show up when she smiled. Not at thirty-nine. Maybe at fifty, when she was old.

"How come you ain't listening to the radio?" he asked her.

"My batteries low," Mama said. "I'ma save 'em up for Sunday morning."

"So you can listen to your church songs?"

"Uh-huh," answered Mama. She closed her eyes and smiled.

Ellis Earl wondered whether she was thinking about when she was much younger and sang in the church choir, as she mentioned it often when she listened to gospel music.

Mama picked up her glass of water from the makeshift table, which was nothing more than an overturned five-gallon lard bucket with a towel draped over it. After taking a few sips of water, she placed the glass back down, ate a few more spoonfuls of beans, then asked Ellis Earl, "Learn anything good in school today?"

"Lots!" he replied.

"Like what?"

Ellis Earl tapped his chin. "Hmm. Let's see." He cast his eyes toward the rain-stained ceiling and thought about his lessons from the day. "Oh!" he said, beaming. "Today Mr. Foster told us about a colored lawyer named Thurgood Marshall. He said he might be the first colored man ever to serve on the Supreme Court."

"Is that right?" said Mama, her face glowing. "I don't know nothin' about all that kind of stuff, but a supreme court sho' do sound real important."

"It is! Mr. Foster said it's one of the highest jobs in the country. About as high as being the president."

"That so?" said Mama.

"Yep," said Ellis Earl. "He said President Johnson said it's about time a colored man was on that court."

"Won't that be nice," said Mama.

"Sure will," said Ellis Earl. "Mr. Foster said that Mr. Thurgood Marshall could help make life better for colored people if he gets a spot on that court."

"We sho' could use some help," said Mama. "Lord knows we needs some help finding jobs."

"You find any work today?"

"A lil' bit. I was able to help Miss Lucinda Butler clean for Mrs. Chalmers this morning. You know Miss Lucinda 'bout as old as black pepper, so she be needing help sometimes."

"I'm glad Mrs. Chalmers let you help out."

"But at half the pay she give Miss Lucinda,"

Mama reminded him. "I didn't have nothin' for the afternoon though. And the boys didn't fare too good today neither," she said, referring to Andre, Aaron, and Raymond. "All three of 'em did some bush-hogging on Mr. Denton's place. He clearin' that big plot of land by the highway to make ready for rice farming. Wasn't able to pay 'em much though. It was so many of 'em out there. White and colored.

"But we oughta have enough to get us some food next week. What Joe brought ain't gon' last long with the babies here."

"When Mr. Thurgood Marshall finds a way to help colored people get real jobs," said Ellis Earl, "you won't have to keep asking white women if their maids need help for the day."

Mama placed her empty plate on the floor, folded her hands in her lap, and rocked slowly in her chair. "Right now I'd just be happy to work regular as anybody's maid. But there just ain't enough white womens needing maids as there is colored womens needing work."

"I wish you didn't have to work as a maid at all," Ellis Earl said quietly.

Mama sighed. "What else is I gon' do?"

Ellis Earl shrugged. "You cook real good."

"Ain't nobody hiring no cooks."

"What about washing?"

"Who I'm gon' wash for besides my own children?"

"You could take in laundry."

"Folks washin' they own clothes, Earl. Times is hard for everybody. For the lil' bit I'm gon' be bringin' in for the time being, I might as well just stay here and help Jeannette with all these children. Only God know when Sylvia gon' have that baby."

"I hope it's soon," said Ellis Earl. "Tonight would be good. That way they can go home next week."

Mama nodded. "I love my grandbabies. But this lil' space we got ain't big enough for the ones already here. Sho' ain't big enough for fo' mo'."

A look of contemplation spread across Ellis Earl's face. "Maybe I can be a lawyer like Mr. Thurgood Marshall when I grow up. I can make a lot of money and buy you a big house."

Mama smiled. "Thought you wanted to be a teacher like Mr. Foster."

"I do," Ellis Earl said. "But I can be a lawyer after that. Or I can be both at the same time."

Ellis Earl couldn't help noticing the sadness in Mama's eyes. "You don't think I can be both?" he asked.

"I do," Mama said wearily. "If you kin finish school."

"Of course I can finish school," said Ellis Earl. "I'm smart enough. I only have two more grades to go before I go to the high school."

"Oh, Earl. You know it ain't 'cause I don't think you smart enough."

"Then what is it?"

"You know we all have to pitch in 'round here to make ends meet," Mama said. "If I need you to work, then you might not be able to even go to the junior high, let alone the high school."

"Mama, please don't say that," Ellis Earl said, tears threatening to spring up. "You know how much I love school."

"I know you do, baby. I want you to finish school and be a teacher or a lawyer, too. But if we git too hungry 'round here, and there be some work that you can do to help out, then school might have to wait."

None of Ellis Earl's older siblings had gone past sixth grade, which he'd always assumed was because they hadn't cared much for school. But he now understood that was not truly the reason why. He looked down at his near-empty bowl and his crumbs of cornbread. If this was all he had to eat every night for the next six years, he would gladly accept it if it meant finishing school.

But he knew the choice wasn't his to make.

The Brown Blues

After supper, and after Beatrice and Deidra had done the dishes, entertainment for the whole family flowed from the middle room. Andre, Aaron, Raymond, and Jeannette, who called themselves the Brown Blues, rehearsed for their future fame as blues singers, just as they did every night.

And as was the younger children's habit every night, they sat on the floor of the front room and swayed and snapped to the beat.

All except Ellis Earl, that is.

Instead of swaying and snapping, he seethed.

He had tried to enjoy listening to his siblings sing. But jealousy got the best of him. He gritted his teeth against the anger rising in him every time he heard Jeannette sing out:

Yo' blues ain't like mines.
Nah, nah, baby.
Yo' blues sho' ain't like mines.

It was not her lack of attention to proper speech that angered Ellis Earl but the fact that she was a girl and singing blues with his brothers. Even though he was only eleven, he thought his brothers should have considered him to sing with them, not Jeannette—the meanest sister who ever lived.

But Ellis Earl, by now, should have been used to being left out by his brothers. For him, it seemed, Oscar was really the only brother he had. Andre, Aaron, and Raymond treated him as though he were one of the girls. "Sissy" is exactly what they called him, as a matter of fact.

The sissy with the chicken legs who couldn't outrun a fish.

The sissy with arms so skinny that he couldn't box a flea.

The sissy whom they wished were sick instead of Oscar.

Although his brothers never said this, Ellis Earl could feel it in his heart. Before Oscar started with all the coughing fits, the fevers, and the weakness of his limbs, he could outrun even fifteen-year-old Raymond by a whole foot when they all lined up to race. Ellis Earl could barely outrun Carrie Ann, and she was a teeny-tiny girl!

Oscar never treated Ellis Earl as poorly as his older brothers did. But Oscar was sick and not much company. So it was just Ellis Earl and the girls—like now—on the floor of the front room, while his older brothers and Jeannette moaned the blues in the middle room.

While Raymond made his old harmonica cry a sad melody, Andre, Aaron, and Jeannette harmonized with their voices:

The blues ain't red, baby,
And the blues ain't pank.
The blues ain't even yellow, honey,
But the blues sho' stank.

"*Pink,*" Ellis Earl muttered to himself. "The word is *pink*. And *pink* rhymes with *stink*, not *stank*."

Carrie Ann, who sat beside him, eyed him sternly and said, "Didn't Mama tell you to stop all that talking to yo'self 'foe you end up in the crazy house?"

Making a dramatic gesture around the room, Ellis Earl retorted, "I'm already in a crazy house."

"Humph," Carrie Ann said. "You 'bout the craziest one of all."

Ellis Earl responded, "You mean the *smartest* one of all."

"I meant what I said. You ain't so smart. You just think you is."

"You won't be saying that when I'm a lawyer one day and making a lot of money."

"I don't care how much money you make. If you keep on mumbling to yo'self, people still gon' think you as crazy as a shot squirrel."

"At least I'll be a rich shot squirrel," Ellis Earl said. "And when I am, I won't give you a dime because you're too mean."

"I won't need no money from you," said Carrie Ann. "I'll have my own. If you kin be a lawyer, then I kin be one, too."

Ellis Earl scoffed. "Girls can't be lawyers. You can be a teacher or a nurse, but not a lawyer."

Carrie Ann crossed her arms and huffed. "And just why not?"

"Because being a lawyer is tough. And girls just ain't tough enough."

Carrie Ann punched him in the arm.

Ellis Earl stifled a howl.

Carrie Ann smirked. "I'm tougher than you or any other boy, Ellis Earl Brown. And if you kin be a lawyer, then I kin be one, too."

SATURDAY, MARCH 18

Not an Occasion for Celebration

THE POUNDING ON THE FRONT DOOR startled Ellis Earl out of a deep sleep. He jerked straight into a sitting position on the mattress. The Hardy Boys mystery *The Secret of the Old Mill* slipped from his chest and slid to the floor. He had been trying to read the book, to no avail, until Mama put out the lamp in the front room.

The front room was now as black as the bottom of one of Mama's old burnt pots. The house was graveyard silent. This was how Ellis Earl knew it was the middle of the night. But what he didn't know, and what confused him greatly, was why someone was banging on the door at this time of night.

Boom. Boom. Boom. Boom. Boom.

The splintered wooden door rattled with each knock. Only a flimsy latch kept it closed. Ellis Earl prayed it wouldn't burst open as it had during a severe thunderstorm.

Mama, bleary-eyed, emerged from the middle room. "Who there?" she called to the door.

"Joseph," came the reply.

"Uncle Joseph?" Ellis Earl whispered.

"Lay back down," Mama ordered him.

Ellis Earl obeyed, but he kept his eyes open.

"What's wrong, Joe?" asked Mama upon opening the door.

Ellis Earl couldn't see him, but he could hear every word his deep-voiced uncle uttered. His tone solemn, he said, "The baby came."

"Thank God," Mama said, sounding relieved. But when she lit the kerosene lamp, she startled.

So did Ellis Earl when he saw the stricken look on Uncle Joseph's face. He realized this was not an occasion for celebration.

Mama clutched her chest. "What's happened, Joe?"

"Things ain't looking good right now." Uncle Joseph glanced over at the mattress where the boys lay. "Them boys all 'sleep?"

"All of 'em but Earl," replied Mama.

Uncle Joseph let out a deep breath. "He a big boy. This ain't too hard for him. Besides, all of 'em gon' know in the morning anyhow."

"The baby a'right?" Mama asked, her voice shaking.

"He a'right," said Uncle Joseph.

"A boy, huh?"

"A big one," Uncle Joseph said, frowning. "Too big."

Mama's hand shot up to her mouth. "Lord."

"The baby a'right," Uncle Joseph said again. "But Sylvia lost a lotta blood. Went into some kinda shock. The doctor sedated her real heavy. Put her in a coma, Junior say."

"A coma?" said Mama, her eyes wide. "I ain't never heard of no such thing as a doctor puttin' nobody in a coma."

By this time, more of the family were emerging from their slumbers. They trickled into the front room, one by one, their faces full of questions.

"Sylvia in a coma." The word passed from person to person.

Jeannette, often careless with her words, said, "At least she ain't dead like Eloise."

The room grew still.

Chills crept along Ellis Earl's arms. The Brown children hardly ever mentioned their oldest sister, Eloise.

Eloise—named after Mama—had been dead for three years. Her death came swiftly when the midwife neglected to stop the bleeding after Ellis Earl's niece Vera was born. This, everyone knew, was the reason for Sylvia's distrust of midwives.

"If they *put* her in a coma," Andre asked, "when is they plannin' on takin' her out of it?"

Uncle Joseph's face seemed to crumple. "She already woke up from it. On her own. Too soon, the doctor say. Now that chile can't see a thing. Not one darn thing. That chile blind as a bat."

MONDAY, MARCH 20

Necessary News for Negro Children

MONDAY DIDN'T COME FAST ENOUGH for Ellis Earl. As he and Carrie Ann piled into Mr. Foster's car with the other seven students, he felt as if he could finally breathe.

Mondays felt normal. The weekends did not. *Especially* this past weekend.

Even though he was scrunched in an automobile with nine other bodies, Ellis Earl usually felt less crowded out than he did at home. But not today. Because as soon as they got in the car and Mr. Foster asked about their weekend, Carrie

Ann started doing what Mama called "flapping her tongue at both ends."

"Sylvia done had her baby!" she blurted out. "Now she blind!"

Mr. Foster tilted the rearview mirror so that Ellis Earl and Carrie Ann were in his sight. Before Ellis Earl could utter a word, Carrie Ann continued, "Something went wrong at the hospital. They put Sylvia in a coma. Now she blind. Pearline and Jewel and Lil' Walt and Prince staying with us till Junior and Sylvia come back to get 'em. We 'on know when that gon' be though, 'specially since Sylvia can't see nothing. We only got a lil' beans in our bowls and we had to have a half peanut butter sammich and rice for supper yesterday 'cause we ran outta beans on Saturday."

Ellis Earl nudged Carrie Ann hard in the side.

"Owww, Earl," she cried. "Stop pokin' me!"

With a strained smile, Mr. Foster adjusted the rearview mirror and pulled the car onto the road. But Larry, who sat on the seat with Ellis Earl and Carrie Ann, stared at them, waiting to hear more.

Encouraged by Larry's inquiring eyes, Carrie Ann gave a complete playback of the entire weekend, giving their little carpool an earful and nearly giving poor Ellis Earl a heart attack from embarrassment. He wished Oscar were with them. Perhaps the two of them together—a nudge (or a slight pinch if necessary) from each side—could have helped Carrie Ann remember Mama's words: *What goes on at the house stays at the house.*

Instead Carrie Ann brought the affairs of the house straight to the carpool:

"Jeannette gave er'body a half-empty bowl of beans . . . We didn't have no cornbread left over for breakfast on Saturday like we used to . . . Pearline peed in the bed, and me and Jeannette and Deidra was mad 'cause we all got wet, too . . . We didn't have nothing to eat on Sunday but the peanut butter sammiches and rice . . . We couldn't go to Big Mama's house and eat 'cause all us wouldn't fit in Uncle Joseph's car . . . I'll be so glad when Sylvia and Junior come get they children . . . I'm hungry. Anybody got some saltine crackers?"

When Mr. Foster's station wagon rolled into the schoolyard, Ellis Earl opened the door before the car came to a complete stop. He couldn't wait to get away from his tell-all little sister. Equally, he couldn't wait to get home and tell Mama that Carrie Ann had been running off at the mouth again, telling all their business. Or, in Mama's words, "airing their dirty laundry"!

Mama is right, Ellis Earl thought. *Carrie Ann is like a bucket with a hole in the bottom. She can't hold nothing! Maybe if Mama took that strap to her like she's been saying, Carrie Ann would learn to keep her big . . . mouth . . . shut!*

But Ellis Earl knew that would probably never happen. Mama was not too quick to use a strap on any of her children, no matter how much she thought they deserved it.

Amid the chaos of his weekend, Ellis Earl had done something that he had never done before (well, maybe once or twice): he had neglected to complete an assignment. It's not that he forgot but that his thoughts were too scattered to concentrate. So there he sat at the very front of Mr. Foster's class, desperately poring over the article that Mr. Foster had assigned to him on Friday with the instructions: "Be prepared on Monday morning to share your thoughts with the class regarding this article."

Mr. Foster and other teachers purchased multiple copies of the weekly *Jet* magazine, clipped articles that they deemed "necessary news for Negro children," and distributed the articles to various students to prepare for a discussion on current events.

Ellis Earl gazed at the article lying atop his open social studies textbook. "Democrats to Bar Discrimination at '68 Convention," the title read. The article was a long one, in Ellis Earl's opinion—too long to read *and* report on in only five minutes. Admittedly, he had at least *skimmed* over the article on Sunday. But with so many of the words unfamiliar to him and without anyone at home to ask for help, Ellis Earl had simply tucked the article back into the front page of his textbook and had forgotten about it until this morning.

Now, with his eyes darting back and forth and his left hand moving his pencil swiftly across his lined paper, the best he could do was jot down the main points and hope to summarize them to his classmates: *subcommittee . . . Democratic National Committee . . . Deep South . . . does not have Negro members . . . should be barred from the party's 1968 national convention . . . President Lyndon B. Johnson . . . sending to Congress new civil rights legislation . . . On the wintry Sunday . . . chief executive told a shivering audience . . . Lincoln began . . . troubled journey towards . . . establishment of a multiracial community . . . President Johnson announced . . . new civil rights program . . . fair housing . . . 1969 . . .*

There, Ellis Earl stopped. Fair housing by 1969? That was only two years away. What exactly was fair housing? he wondered. Is it possible that he and his family could live in a real house by the time he turned thirteen? Would he and Oscar have a real bed? Would they have a bedroom? Could the president of the United States make that happen? If the president could get a colored man on the Supreme Court, then maybe that man, Mr. Thurgood Marshall, could help colored people get fair housing.

A smile formed at the thought.

Ellis Earl wasn't sure what that other stuff in the article meant. He had never heard of a Democratic National Convention, nor was he certain of what the word *subcommittee* meant. But he did understand the words *Deep South* and most certainly *Negro*, because that was what he was: a Negro living in the Deep South.

After his oral presentation, the class applauded him, but not Mr. Foster. "Mr. Brown," he said, stopping Ellis Earl before he sat down. "There was one sentence in that article that I hoped you would take note of and share with the class."

Ellis Earl scanned the article again. What had he left out? He had mentioned how President Johnson wanted to make sure Negroes were represented at this Democratic National Convention next year. He had mentioned how President Johnson wanted to carry on the work that Abraham Lincoln had begun over a hundred years ago and help the United States become a multiracial community. He had mentioned that President Johnson wanted fair housing for Negroes. He had even mentioned that the president had a whole package of civil rights bills that he wanted to pass. What had he missed?

After he had scanned the article twice, he peered up at Mr. Foster and admitted, "I don't know what I'm missing, sir."

Mr. Foster replied, "Sit down. Read over the article and find two words that are of utmost importance to my mission here at this school."

Two words that are of utmost importance to my mission here at this school. Though annoyed, Ellis Earl managed to control the huff that wanted to escape him. Mr. Foster should have said up front that he wanted him to look for two words that were important to *him*. Ellis Earl had homed in on the two words, *fair* and *housing*, that were to his benefit instead.

"Let's have our next article while we wait," said Mr. Foster.

A girl named Cassandra Smith stood. "'WEALTHY WHITE FAMILY BEFRIENDS NEGRO IN BIASED INDIANA CITY,'" she read loudly from her prepared notes. Some of the children covered their ears because Cassandra always spoke louder than necessary. "This story is about a Negro woman named Mrs. Nellie B. Kanno," Cassandra continued, nearly shouting. "Mrs. Kanno moved to Michigan City, Indiana, last year in 1966."

Cassandra looked up from her paper. "Ain't it kinda strange that the city is called Michigan City, but it ain't in Michigan?"

When none of her peers responded, Cassandra shrugged and began reading from her notes again. "When Mrs. Kanno and her husband moved to Michigan City, they was expecting bad things to happen to them because Michigan City used to be where the Ku Klux Klan had a stronghold." With furrowed brows Cassandra added, "I don't know what that word mean, but it sound bad. And scary."

The class laughed.

Satisfied that she had now gotten the kind of attention she desired, Cassandra smiled and continued. "Mrs. Kanno's husband's name is Ayalew. He is a African from Ethiopia. He went to Indiana to complete his college degree and get a P-H-D."

Laughter interrupted Cassandra's presentation again as everyone thought she was attempting to rhyme when she said "degree" and "P-H-D."

"Mrs. Kanno was looking for a job as a . . ." Cassandra paused.

"Yes?" said Mr. Foster, his brows raised.

"I don't know how to say this word: *c-o-u-n-s-e-l-o-r*."

"Counselor," said Mr. Foster.

"Thank you," said Cassandra. "Mrs. Kanno was looking for a job as a counselor. And she was looking for a place to stay. But everywhere she went, they told her, 'No colored.' Or they lied to her and said, 'The place done already been rented.'"

Cassandra took a deep breath. "Mrs. Kanno was getting real fed up and mad about all this. Then one day she met some rich white people. They was named Frederick and Marion Pilliard. They said that Mrs. Kanno and her husband could live with them in they big fancy house."

A few *wows* came from the class.

"Mrs. Kanno didn't trust them at first. She said, 'Why these white people want me to come stay with them? Why they doing this? Ain't they scared they gon' lose they white friends?' But she found out that Mr. Pilliard 'n 'em had been trying to help colored people all the time. They had helped a lot of colored people in Michigan City, and they helped Mrs. Kanno get a good job."

Cassandra looked up from her notes, smiled at the class, and said, "That's all." Oddly, she said this last part quietly.

The class applauded, and Cassandra took her seat.

"What did we learn from Miss Smith's presentation?" asked Mr. Foster.

A girl named Deborah Walker raised her hand. Mr. Foster nodded permission to speak.

"We learned that all white people don't hate colored people," said Deborah. "Some of them want to help."

"Correct," said Mr. Foster.

Another hand went up.

"Mr. Greene," said Mr. Foster.

Willie Greene, who had a deep baritone voice even though he was only twelve years old, said, "We learnt that Mississippi ain't the only place where white folks is mean. And we learnt that Michigan City ain't in Michigan."

The class erupted in giggles.

With a stern look, Mr. Foster rapped on his desk with his wooden paddle. The class promptly calmed down.

"Thank you for your opinion, Mr. Greene," he said. "But that was not the point of the article. We are all well aware that racism exists all over the country. The point of the article, as Miss Walker has stated, is that not all white people despise the Negro race. There are some who want to see us advance."

With a sheepish glance toward Mr. Foster, Willie Greene offered his apology to the class for his attempt to be comedic.

Ellis Earl, in the meantime, had not taken long to figure out what Mr. Foster wanted of him as far as his article was concerned. For as soon as he had observed the page, the two words which he knew would be of utmost importance to Mr. Foster seemed to stare back at him:

Black. Power.

Ellis Earl hadn't actually heard Mr. Foster use the two words together, but he had heard him speak often enough about a group called the Black Panthers. He spoke about how some people were afraid of how powerful the Panthers were. And though Mr. Foster wasn't a member of the group, he told his students that his mission was to have the same type of impact in his community as the Black Panthers had in theirs.

Ellis Earl's face lit up with a grin when Mr. Foster asked him, "You ready, Mr. Brown?"

"Yes, sir, I'm ready."

Although he wasn't sure how to pronounce some of the words, Ellis Earl stood and read the quote: "'Lincoln began his troubled journey towards a new concept which would go beyond theories of black power—beyond the ancient blunders of racism to the establishment of a multiracial community—in which a man's pride in his racial origins would be wholly consistent with his commitment to the common endeavor.'"

"Meaning?" asked Mr. Foster.

Again Ellis Earl floundered. He read the quote again silently.

He wanted to say something—to get this thing right. He knew the words *black power* were significant to his teacher, but he didn't know how to summarize the words from the article. He didn't even know what some of the words, like *theories* and *endeavor*, meant. He felt like a failure as a trickle of sweat suddenly rolled from his armpits and down his sides—something that often happened when he was nervous.

Nearly in tears, he swallowed hard and said, "I don't know what it means."

With a look of concern rather than disappointment, Mr. Foster relegated Ellis Earl to his seat. He scanned the room. "Would anyone else like to tell us what this quote means?"

The hand of Philip, Ellis Earl's friend, shot up.

After getting Mr. Foster's permission to speak, Philip said, "What I think President Lyndon B. Johnson means, sir, is that President Abraham Lincoln didn't just want the slave owners to free the slaves, but he wanted everyone to get along after the war. He wanted everyone to be treated the same. And he wanted Black people to be proud of who they were even if they used to be slaves."

"Does everyone agree?" Mr. Foster inquired of the class.

A resounding "Yes, sir" came from the class.

Ellis Earl felt his face grow hot. How could Philip call himself his friend, then embarrass him like that? He wanted to defend himself. He wanted to show Mr. Foster that he, too, was smart.

He raised his hand.

Mr. Foster acknowledged him. "Mr. Brown, you have a question?"

"I have a comment, sir," Ellis Earl answered.

"You may proceed," replied Mr. Foster.

With a serious expression, Ellis Earl said, "Philip said 'Black people.' The article said 'Negro people.' He should have said what the article said."

"Oh?" said Mr. Foster, his brows raised. "Does the class agree?"

Before anyone could answer, Philip defended himself. "My cousin Kareem said we shouldn't call ourselves Negroes and colored people anymore. We're Black people, like our brothers and sisters in Africa. And we should be proud of that."

Angrily, Ellis Earl said, "You should've said what was in the article."

"We should call ourselves Black people," Philip said proudly. "Negro and colored are names other people called us. Black is what we can call ourselves. Black is our ancestors. Black is us. Black is power."

Ellis Earl let out a deep breath. "But the article—"

"—did indeed use the word *black*, as you yourself pointed out," Mr. Foster interrupted him. "So Mr. Harris is correct in his use of the word. There is no sense in being controversial simply for the sake of controversy, Mr. Brown."

Ellis Earl sank down in his seat, defeated. When he dared to glance over at his friend, Philip frowned and looked the other way.

Carrie Ann isn't the only one who should have kept her mouth shut this morning, thought Ellis Earl. *Looks like my big mouth just cost me a friend.*

A Closed Mouth

THE LUNCH THAT MR. FOSTER shared with his students that day almost made up for the humiliation Ellis Earl had caused himself. *Almost.*

And now, even more embarrassing, Ellis Earl wanted so badly to lick his fingers while he devoured the perfectly seasoned drumsticks and buttered biscuits that Mr. Foster had placed before him. But he dared not, for fear that Mr. Foster would catch him and whack him across the knuckles with the wooden ruler, as had happened the previous week to a rather tall boy named Dale Harper. Ellis Earl could hardly blame him; it was hard not to lick one's fingers when the chicken was so juicy.

As he sat in the classroom with the other seven students with whom Mr. Foster shared his lunch that day, Ellis Earl couldn't help but feel sorry for Carrie Ann. Other teachers brought lunches to share with their students, but Carrie Ann's teacher was not one of them. Carrie Ann, however, was able to convince two or more of her fellow classmates to share their lunches with her. In Mama's words, *Carrie Ann could coax a nestful of eggs from a barren hen.* Yet what she rounded up could never compare to the lunches Mr. Foster brought.

Oscar, too, when he was in school, always found a way to secure himself a lunch by collecting bits of food from those around him—*when* those around him had food, that is.

Now Oscar would have to suffer like the rest of Ellis Earl's family. On good days, there would be something in the house that Jeannette could rummage up to prepare a midday meal. But today was not a good day. There was little hope that there would be anything for them to eat before suppertime, especially with four extra little ones at the house.

Ellis Earl tried to concentrate on his lessons and not think about his family when he was at school, but he couldn't help feeling guilty to have food when they didn't. He peeked toward the back of the classroom, where Mr. Foster kept a large sack containing the lunch he brought. *There had to be more biscuits and chicken in that sack,* Ellis Earl thought. There were only seven of them eating today when there were usually ten or eleven. Surely Mr. Foster had brought enough to feed at least twelve people. He was resourceful in that way. *What will he do with the leftover food?* Ellis Earl wondered.

After thoroughly scrubbing every trace of the fried chicken from his fingers with his handkerchief, Ellis Earl timidly rose from his seat and approached Mr. Foster's desk. Mr. Foster, who himself was not eating, gazed down, lost in the book he was reading.

To Ellis Earl, it appeared that he didn't want to be bothered.

Suddenly a lump that really did feel about as round as a frog found its way to Ellis Earl's throat. When he cleared it, Mr. Foster looked up. Using his finger to mark the page, he closed his book. "How may I help you, Mr. Brown?"

Ellis Earl, remembering what Mr. Foster always told his students, stood tall, squared his shoulders, and prepared to project his voice with strength. Instead it came out in a squeak. "Sir," he said. Then his voice caught in his throat again.

"Speak up, young man," Mr. Foster urged him.

Ellis Earl next remembered the words Uncle Joseph often told Mama when she refused to let him know her family needed food: *A closed mouth don't get fed.* With that thought, Ellis Earl gestured toward the back of the classroom, where the sack rested on the table. "That was a very delicious lunch you provided for us today, sir."

Mr. Foster smiled broadly. "Why, thank you, Mr. Brown," he said.

Ellis Earl winced. Those were not the words he meant to say. Why couldn't he be brave like Oscar? Oscar would not have hesitated to speak up and look out for his siblings. He might have been eleven months younger than Ellis Earl, but he was twelve months bolder. Sometimes Ellis Earl wondered why it was he, and not Oscar, who was so fortunate to be in Mr. Foster's presence. Oscar would have had the courage *daily* to ask Mr. Foster for food to take home.

Do it for Oscar, Ellis Earl pleaded with himself. *He would do it for you.*

"If you have leftovers, I wouldn't mind taking them off your hands, sir," he continued, a slight shake in his voice. "I could take them home with me and share with Oscar. You know—he's still sick. And with my little sisters, too, if you have enough."

Ellis Earl's heart sank when a sad expression came upon Mr. Foster's face. "I'm sorry, Mr. Brown," he said. "But the leftovers are already spoken for."

Though Mr. Foster had tried to be discreet, Ellis Earl still noticed his quick glance toward two boys sitting near the window. One was Dale Harper, the boy who had gotten his fingers whacked for licking them. The other was Dale's friend Willie Greene. Ellis Earl felt a pang of jealousy toward Dale because Dale didn't have any siblings, so he wouldn't need to split up the food he took home. But he had empathy for Willie, a terribly skinny boy whom he knew to have as many siblings as he and no father at home to help his mother care for them.

From his desk, Mr. Foster retrieved a folded piece of paper and placed it in his book to mark the page where he had stopped reading. He set the book on his desk, intertwined his fingers in front of him, and leaned in toward Ellis Earl. "Is there anything else I could help you with, Mr. Brown?"

Ellis Earl bit his bottom lip and hesitated. Mr. Foster asked him this question often, and Ellis Earl always told him no. Yet there was so much he wanted to share with his teacher. He wanted to tell him about how crowded out he felt at home—suffocated by so many people—yet he still felt alone. He felt different. *And* he *wanted* to be different.

He wanted to be like Mr. Foster.

Mr. Julius Foster, a graduate of Alcorn College, was a refined and handsome man with smooth, bronze-tone skin and dark brown eyes. He had wavy jet-black hair, with the same number of waves in it every day. Ellis Earl knew this because he'd counted them. He'd once tried to make his own hair wavy. But it was too thick and kinky.

It was not just how Mr. Foster looked or how he carried himself that Ellis Earl admired. It was what he *did*.

Ellis Earl wanted to bring a huge sack of food to school each day and share it with others. He wanted his family to have their own car to ride in rather than always having to get word to someone to pick them up or to wait until someone *showed up* to take them where they needed to go. He wanted money so that he could go into town and buy a new pair of shoes, a new pair of pants, a new shirt, a new pair of BVD underwear instead of the two holey, worn-out pairs he alternated wearing each day. Even a real toothbrush with real toothpaste would have been nice. It certainly would have beat putting salt on his finger and rubbing it over his teeth every morning.

These are the things he wanted to tell Mr. Foster. But he couldn't. Carrie Ann had already talked too much on the way to school. Mama wouldn't be happy if he, too, began running off at the mouth. So Ellis Earl remained silent. He'd already put himself out on a ledge, as Mama would say, to inquire about the extra food. There was no sense in venturing all the way to the end and risking slipping over.

Seeing that he didn't wish to confide in him, Mr. Foster said, "Tell me again what it is you wish to do with your life when you grow up. Teacher, was it? Or was that Mr. Harris who wanted to be a teacher?" He nodded toward Philip.

Relieved that Mr. Foster had changed the subject, Ellis Earl released his breath. "We both want to be teachers, sir," he answered. "I want to teach social studies and science, and Philip wants to teach mathematics. But I've been thinking," Ellis Earl said, shifting his feet, "I might want to be a lawyer, like Mr. Thurgood Marshall."

Mr. Foster raised his brows. "Is that so?"

"Yes, sir," Ellis Earl said, nodding. "I wouldn't mind being both. But I wonder if I could be a lawyer and help colored people get fair housing like I read about in the article today."

"You have the potential to be anything that you want to be, Mr. Brown," Mr. Foster answered, eyeing him sternly. "But you must be prepared to work hard whether you want to be either a teacher *or* a lawyer. And you'll have to speak up more."

Ellis Earl thought about his argument with Carrie Ann over the weekend. "Can girls be lawyers?" he asked.

"Of course," said Mr. Foster. "Why do you ask?"

Ellis Earl shrugged. "It's nothing. Carrie Ann said she wanted to be a lawyer. But she only said it because she was copying me."

"I think Carrie Ann would make a great lawyer," said Mr. Foster. "She certainly has the gift of gab."

"What's gab?"

"It means she's not afraid to speak up," said Mr. Foster. "Maybe she'll be like Miss Marian Wright, traveling to Washington, DC, speaking on behalf of poor folks in Mississippi."

"Who's Miss Marian Wright?"

"Someone very smart. The first Black woman to practice law in Mississippi."

"She went all the way to Washington, DC?"

Mr. Foster nodded. "And she's trying to convince Washington, DC, to come to Mississippi."

When Ellis Earl's face twisted in confusion, Mr. Foster chuckled. "Not the city, Mr. Brown. The politicians. Miss Wright attended a Senate subcommittee hearing last week and told the senators that folks here in Mississippi were having a hard time putting food on the table. They didn't believe her, so she asked the senators to come see for themselves."

Ellis Earl felt a wave of embarrassment sweep over him. Even though Mama had said that times were hard for everybody, he couldn't help feeling ashamed to hear his teacher acknowledge the fact while he stood there begging for food. He swallowed his shame and asked, "Are they coming?"

"Well, rumor has it that a couple of them might," said Mr. Foster. "One being Senator Robert Kennedy."

"Who's that?"

"He's the younger brother of John F. Kennedy."

He had heard of John F. Kennedy. His uncle Joseph even had a large photograph of the man he called "JFK" hanging on his front room wall. Beyond the fact that he had been the president and that he had gotten assassinated, Ellis Earl didn't know much else about him.

"My uncle has a picture of President Kennedy on his wall," he told Mr. Foster. "Is that because he got killed?"

"Perhaps," answered Mr. Foster. "But many Black people around here believe President Kennedy was a fighter for equal rights, like what you talked about in your article this morning."

"What about his brother? He fighting for equal rights, too?"

Mr. Foster smiled. "Let's hope so."

"Don't we already have senators in Mississippi? How come they need to come all the way from Washington, DC?"

"We do have senators," said Mr. Foster, nodding. "John Stennis and James Eastland. They also believe that Miss Wright is exaggerating."

Ellis Earl wasn't sure what the word *exaggerating* meant, but even without looking it up in the dictionary on Mr. Foster's desk, he figured it meant that the senators thought Miss Wright was making things up. He thought about his siblings and nieces and nephews at home. With nine of them there today, they would be lucky to each eat a biscuit before suppertime, and that's only because Uncle Joseph had brought over the small amount of groceries on Friday. There were days when they had nothing at all to eat. Uncle Joseph had his own family to feed and couldn't always help feed his sister's large family, too.

"Why do the senators think she's exaggerating?" asked Ellis Earl.

With a frown, Mr. Foster said, "Because they choose to, Mr. Brown. It's easy for them to ignore poverty when they don't have to see it every day."

"But what can the senators do about people not having food?"

"There are programs to help people get food," said Mr. Foster.

"My uncle told my mama about something called food stamps. She said she tried to get them three times already, and she wasn't gonna try no more—I mean *any*more. She said they only let white people get the food stamps. They made it easy for white people to get them but made it hard for colored people to get them."

With a frown, Mr. Foster said, "That's what Miss Wright is fighting for. She wants to make sure all people have access to those programs, especially here in the Delta."

"That's very nice of her," said Ellis Earl. "I didn't know lawyers did things like that. And I didn't know that girls—I mean ladies—could be lawyers." He suddenly felt poorly for having told Carrie Ann she couldn't be a lawyer. But he wasn't so sure that he would tell her that she could be one either. The last thing he wanted to hear was Carrie Ann saying, "Told ya!"

"A lawyer, huh?" asked Mr. Foster. He nodded toward his bookshelf lined along the wall. "Which reading choices have you been making lately?"

Again Ellis Earl hesitated. Mr. Foster often indicated that he should read more challenging books if he wanted to continue to excel in his studies past grammar school. But Ellis Earl was ashamed to admit that he found those books intimidating. So many words, and so few pictures! Just like that Hardy Boys mystery, *The Secret of the Old Mill*, his friend Philip had suggested. Regardless of how hard he tried, Ellis Earl simply couldn't keep up with the story of the two boys helping their father solve a mystery.

As soon as he made it to the classroom that morning, he had slipped the book back on the shelf, then avoided Philip all morning in case he asked about it. It seemed that Philip was able to devour a Hardy Boys mystery as quickly as Ellis Earl was able to devour Mr. Foster's lunch. Ellis Earl wished he could do the same.

But he preferred to read the books that he took home to his younger siblings, fun books like *Curious George* and *Hop on Pop*. But he knew those books wouldn't help him improve his vocabulary the way Mr. Foster said he needed to before going to the junior high school next year. Assuming he'd even get to go to junior high.

Ellis Earl chose to be honest with his teacher. "I haven't been reading the books you recommended." He cast his sight on the floor and mumbled, "I've been reading the books that you allow me to take home to share with my little sisters and niece."

Leaning forward, Mr. Foster clasped his hands together and rested them under his chin. "So you prefer books with pictures?"

Without looking up, Ellis Earl nodded.

"Eye contact, Mr. Brown," said Mr. Foster. "And use your voice."

Ellis Earl raised his eyes to meet Mr. Foster's. He straightened his shoulders and answered, "Yes, sir."

"I think I might have a book for you," said Mr. Foster. "I picked it up over the weekend while visiting my parents in Jackson." He retrieved his briefcase from beneath his desk, reached in, and pulled out a book. "A church donated a box of brand-new books to the high school where my mother teaches. Some of the books are a bit young for Mother's students."

Ellis Earl couldn't imagine being able to focus on a book that someone thought suitable for students in high school. But not wanting to disappoint his teacher, he reached for the book.

Mr. Foster held it back. "Clean hands?"

Ellis Earl showed him his hands.

Mr. Foster gave him the book.

Ellis Earl studied the cover.

"'Charlie and the Chocolate Factory,'" he read aloud.

He turned to the first page. He was delighted to see pictures. He was even more delighted as he scanned the first few pages. The boy's name was Charlie Bucket, which Ellis Earl thought was funny. And he lived in a small house with only two rooms—a house smaller than Ellis Earl's. He shared the house with six grown-ups. And they had only one bed. Ellis Earl's family had two.

"Wow," Ellis Earl whispered.

"I thought of you when I saw it," said Mr. Foster. "Think you might like to read it? If so, it's yours to keep."

Ellis Earl nodded shyly but quickly remembered his earlier admonishment. "Yes, I think I might like this book, sir," he answered, speaking loudly and clearly.

But what he wanted to say was:

Charlie's family sounds like mine.

Their house sounds like mine.

But he held his peace. He wanted to be brave like Oscar and speak up more. But not just yet.

He was still not quite ready to disclose too many details of his paltry life to his princely teacher.

Instead he stared again at the cover of the book. The picture of the chocolate bar made his mouth water, but more importantly, the subtitle piqued his interest. It said the story was about four nasty children, a hero, and Mr. Wonka.

Ellis Earl squinted at Mr. Foster. "Is Charlie one of the four nasty children or the hero?"

Mr. Foster shrugged. "What do you think?"

"The hero?" asked Ellis Earl. "Since the book is named after him?"

"That's probably a safe bet," said Mr. Foster.

Ellis Earl smiled. *A hero. Maybe I can learn how to be one, too.*

TUESDAY, MARCH 21

Save the Cat

"COME ON, CARRIE ANN," Ellis Earl pleaded. "We gotta get home."

Carrie Ann shook her head. "Nuh-uh. I ain't goin' nowhere. Not long as that cat standing there."

The mangy yellow cat stood by the side of the road. He stared at the Brown siblings. Rather than running away, he seemed mesmerized by Carrie Ann's refusal to cross the same path that he had just crossed.

At first, Ellis Earl hadn't noticed the cat. He was too busy trying to walk and read at the same time. He had never been this captivated by a book. He hated that he had to stop for something as trivial as convincing Carrie Ann to move past a cat.

"It ain't gonna hurt you," said Ellis Earl. "So come on." He grabbed his sister by the wrist and yanked her forward.

Carrie Ann yanked back. "I ain't worried 'bout him hurtin' me. I'm worried 'bout him bringin' me bad luck!"

"It's yellow," said Ellis Earl. "A black cat is bad luck, and only if it crosses to the left. This cat crossed to the right, so it wouldn't cause bad luck even if it *was* black."

"All cats is bad luck."

"Are," corrected Ellis Earl.

"What?"

"All cats *are* bad luck."

"That's what I just said!"

"No, I meant—Oh, never mind! Even if that cat was as black as midnight, it couldn't bring us no more bad luck than we already have."

Ellis Earl began naming off the bad luck. "Oscar's sick. The icebox is empty. Spring is taking her time getting here, and we're about to run out of wood. Sylvia's blind and can't take care of her own children, so we don't know how long the house is gonna be packed—"

Carrie Ann cut him off. "Them lil' children don't take up *that* much space, Earl. And at least Sylvia's sister keeping the baby. We wouldn't git *no* sleep if a lil' hollin' baby was around."

"Well, we still got a lotta bad luck," said Ellis Earl. "And I don't think that cat can bring us one ounce more."

With that, he spun on his heels and headed home.

Carrie Ann cried, "You gon' leave me here with this ugly cat, Ellis Earl Brown?"

Without one peek back, Ellis Earl replied, "Yup."

"Humph!" said Carrie Ann. But she still didn't move. Instead she tried shooing away the cat. "Go on, you! Find somebody else to give yo' bad luck to."

"Will you just come on, girl?" Ellis Earl called over his shoulder. "Only black cats are bad luck. Maybe this yellow one can bring us some good luck."

"Oh, all right!" Carrie Ann conceded. "But if somethin' bad happen to us, don't blame me." She side-eyed the pitiful yellow cat. "That ugly cat just crossed over this here path. Now we 'bout to cross in the same spot. If that ain't bad luck, then I don't know what is."

"Having to walk home with a stubborn little sister like you every day is," Ellis Earl grumbled.

"You callin' me bad luck?"

Ellis Earl exhaled a bottled-up sigh. "Just drop it, Carrie Ann. The cat ain't bad luck, and you ain't either."

To Carrie Ann's chagrin, when they began moving along the path, the cat followed.

Carrie Ann spun around. "No!" With a wagging finger, she warned, "You *can't* follow us home."

"Meow," the cat replied, as if pleading with Carrie Ann to allow him to follow.

"Fine," said Carrie Ann, irritated. "Come on to the house with us then. But don't expect nothing to eat. Not even a saucer of milk, 'cause we ain't got none."

"Meow," the cat said again, this time as if to say, *Thank you.*

By the time they reached the house, Carrie Ann had fallen in love. The first thing she did when she burst through the front door was to announce to their younger siblings that *she* had a cat.

Unfortunately for her, Jeannette was sitting in the front room, braiding Beatrice's hair while the other girls—Deidra, Jewel, Vera, and Pearline—sat on the floor in order by age, awaiting their turns to have their freshly washed Afro puffs twisted into cornrows.

"You better take that cat back wherever you found it," said Jeannette. "We ain't runnin' no save-the-cat charity here. We got enough mouths to feed already. Sho' ain't 'bout to split up the little we have with no darn animal."

Carrie Ann shrugged. "I already told him we ain't got no food for him. He followed us home anyway. Earl said he ain't bad luck."

Jeannette's eyes bugged. "You brought a black cat to this house?"

Ellis Earl placed his books on the cinder block in the corner, then eased over to the mattress where Oscar lay. "It's a yellow cat," he said. "Or maybe orange. It's kinda mangy-looking, so I can't really tell."

Jeannette stopped mid-braid. "Y'all brought a mangy cat to this house?"

"A cat?" asked Oscar. He raised himself up on

one elbow. "You brought us a cat?" he asked Ellis Earl, his face lighting up.

"We didn't bring it. It followed us home."

"Well, walk back down the road and make it follow you back where it came from," said Jeannette. "We don't need no fleas 'round here."

"I don't think he got fleas," said Carrie Ann. "He wasn't scratching or nothing."

Jeannette frowned. "You didn't touch that cat, did you, Earl? I don't want you 'round Oscar if you did."

Ellis Earl raised his hands, palms out. "I didn't touch it."

"Me neither," said Carrie Ann.

"Well, go git the broom and shoo that thing away from here," she told Carrie Ann.

"I wanna keep him," Carrie Ann said.

"Me too," said Oscar.

All the little ones joined in with their "me too"s.

"Y'all ain't keepin' no cat," Jeannette said.

"I'll ask Mama," Ellis Earl said. "She'll let us keep it."

"Mama ain't here," said Jeannette. "I'm in charge."

"Where she at?" asked Ellis Earl. "I thought she wasn't going out to work till the little children left."

Jeannette went back to braiding Beatrice's hair. "Aaron got word yesterday that Miss Lucinda down sick with the flu or something. Mama went to town this morning to work for Mrs. Chalmers till Miss Lucinda get better. So I'm back in charge. Now go git that broom."

"Humph!" said Carrie Ann. She turned and stormed toward the kitchen, grumbling the entire way.

"Mama got a job?" Ellis Earl asked.

Jeannette stopped working the magic with her fingers and scowled at him. "Didn't I just say she went in this morning to take Miss Lucinda's place?"

Ellis Earl's heart sank. He was glad that his mama would make some money, but he surely wished she didn't have to scrounge about for it.

Jeannette chastised him. "Stop looking all pitiful. Ain't no shame in cleaning folks' houses as long as they paying you for it."

"Pennies," Ellis Earl muttered.

"That's better than nothing," Jeannette said, glaring at him. "You'll understand when you have to get out there and look for work."

"I'm finishing school," Ellis Earl said. "I'm gonna be a lawyer."

Jeannette snorted. "Be a cold day in hell 'foe that happen."

"Then the devil better buy a coat," said Ellis Earl.

When Carrie Ann returned with the broom, Ellis Earl offered to help her shoo the cat back down the road.

"I can do it by myself," said Carrie Ann. "It's my cat."

"That ain't yo' cat," said Jeannette. "That's Nature's cat, and it's called a stray." She told Ellis Earl, "Go out there and make sho' she run that nasty cat on 'way from here."

When Oscar slumped back down on the mattress and began to weep, Ellis Earl pleaded with Jeannette. "Can't we keep it for Oscar? Me and Carrie Ann will clean it up real good."

With her lips thinned into a frown, Jeannette shook her head and pointed toward the door.

"I don't need yo' help, Ellis Earl," Carrie Ann said when Ellis Earl followed her to the porch.

With sad eyes, the cat stared up at them from the bottom of the porch steps.

Carrie Ann stared back at him.

So did Ellis Earl.

Normally Ellis Earl Brown was not a disobedient child. But today he rationalized with himself that his fourteen-year-old sister, Jeannette, was not really a grown-up, even if she acted like one *and* even if she was officially in charge of the little children while Mama was working. He considered the fact that the look in his younger sister's eyes said she really didn't want to use that broom to shoo the miserable-looking cat away. He considered the fact that the look in the cat's eyes said he didn't want to be sent away. And most importantly, he considered the fact that Oscar, probably more than Carrie Ann, didn't want the cat to be sent away.

He glanced back at the house and noticed Oscar peeking from behind the curtain. How it made his heart ache to see his sick brother longing for something as simple as a stray cat. Oscar didn't ask for much. None of them did. Plus, Oscar had a birthday coming up, and Ellis Earl knew the odds that he would be able to get him something, regardless of his promise, were slim. The least he could do was save the cat for him.

"Come on," he told Carrie Ann. "We'll walk up

the road a piece, then let the cat follow us back. Jeannette will think we sent him away."

Carrie Ann beamed. "We kin keep him?"

"For Oscar," Ellis Earl said. "But don't tell no one. Not a soul. You hear me?"

Carrie Ann traced a cross on her chest with her finger. "Cross my heart and hope to die. I promise not to tell nobody."

"Good. I'll tell Oscar when we go to bed. Don't tell the other little children either. Wouldn't want them to start blabbering to Jeannette."

"Can we name him Lucky? Maybe he the reason Mama got that job."

"I don't care what you call him. Call him Yellow Cat if you want. Just don't tell Jeannette that we didn't shoo him away."

Carrie Ann crossed her heart again. "I promise," she said, her face serious. "I won't tell a soul."

WEDNESDAY, MARCH 22

Marching Over Nonsense

"'COPS CAUSE B'HAM CHILDREN to Cringe with Fear,'" a boy named Jerry Jones read with more emotion than Ellis Earl thought necessary. "'Civil rights leaders in Birmingham, Alabama, said that the increasing number of Negroes who have been killed by the police in the city—ten within the past fourteen months—is causing alarm in the Negro community and children now 'cringe' with fear at the sight of the police.'"

Though the topic was serious, several of the students giggled when Jerry shivered dramatically as he said the word *cringe*. Mr. Foster shushed them as Jerry continued. "'Civic groups asked the law enforcement officials there to stop the dual methods—apprehend the whites, shoot the Negroes pattern—that have caused the death of at least ten Negroes within fourteen months in their community—'"

"You just said that," interrupted Dale Harper, who had a habit of speaking before being acknowledged.

"Talk to the folks who made the magazine," said Jerry. "They wrote it twice."

The same group of gigglers giggled again.

Mr. Foster gave the entire class a stern look. "If some of you feel you must disrespect our speaker by not giving him your full attention, may I suggest you sit in the hallway and wait for Principal Cooper to pass by with his paddle."

The class quieted down, and Jerry read, "'The letter to high officials said that policemen must not be considered judge, jury, and executioner.'"

After the class allowed Jerry to finish his article, Mr. Foster opened the floor for discussion. He began with a question: "Besides demonstrating in the streets as the citizens of Birmingham are doing, what else can be done to help solve the problem of police brutality against Negroes?"

"Negroes kin quit actin' a fool and gittin' arrested!" said Dale, the boy who had interrupted Jerry earlier.

Ellis Earl's friend Philip disagreed. "You're missing the whole point of the article," he said. "It's not about whether or not Black people get arrested or don't get arrested. It's about how the police arrest white people differently than how they arrest Black people. Like the article said, whites are *apprehended*. Blacks are shot."

Dale scoffed. "*Apprehended?* What do that even mean?"

"Arrested, fool," said Jerry.

"Respect," reminded Mr. Foster.

"Well, he ain't very respectful," Jerry countered.

"Keep this up, and you will both be in the hallway," said Mr. Foster.

"Yes, sir," muttered Jerry.

"Like the article said," continued Philip, "the community is asking the police to approach all people the same way whether they are white or Black. They shouldn't arrest one race and shoot the other. If people don't protest, then nothing will ever be done about it. The police will think this discrimination between the races is acceptable. Black people will continue getting killed instead of being apprehended the way white people are."

"Excellent, Mr. Harris," said Mr. Foster.

Ellis Earl was surprised that, after Philip, a girl named Cora raised her hand. Cora rarely raised her hand, usually speaking only when called upon by Mr. Foster. But on those few occasions when she did speak, Ellis Earl's heart fluttered, for Cora had one of the most beautiful voices he had ever heard.

But today Ellis Earl would not have the pleasure of hearing Cora speak. As soon as Mr. Foster acknowledged her, a few girls in the back of the room snickered. Cora put her hand down and said, "Never mind," so quietly that she could barely be heard.

"If there is something you would like to share with the class, Miss Scott, please do so," encouraged Mr. Foster.

Cora only shook her head.

Mr. Foster pointed at the back of the classroom from where the snickers had come. "That entire section will be staying in for recess today," he said.

Groans replaced the snickers.

Inspired by Cora and remembering what Mr. Foster had said about speaking up more, Ellis Earl raised his hand to make a comment about the article. "The article is also about how scared the children are of the police," he said after Mr. Foster acknowledged him. "I would be scared, too, if the police in our town shot colored people instead of arresting them."

"But they criminals," interrupted a girl named Betty King. "Why should people be marching in the streets for them? Didn't nobody march in the streets when my cousin got kilt at a dice game last year. But if the police had busted up the dice game and kilt him, people care all of a sudden? 'Cause the police kilt him 'stead of another Negro?"

"Yes," Philip said bluntly.

"That's. So. Stupid," said Betty. "If a colored person get kilt by the police while they getting arrested, people march in the streets. If a colored person get kilt *on the streets* by another colored person, folks don't do nothing but cry."

As the class grew silent, Ellis Earl allowed both sides of the argument to work through his brain. He wanted to continue adding to the conversation as Philip had done. After his thoughts settled, he nervously raised his hand.

"Yes, Mr. Brown?"

"I have a question for Betty," said Ellis Earl, turning to Betty. "Did the person who killed your cousin at the dice game get arrested?"

"'Course he did," answered Betty.

"Did he go to jail?" asked Ellis Earl.

Betty scoffed. "You think they just let him go or something? Yeah, he went to jail. Still there."

"So why would people need to march in the streets?" asked Ellis Earl. "The person who killed your cousin went to jail like he was supposed to. But what if the police had *killed* the man instead of arresting him? How would *that* make you feel?"

Betty shrugged. "Why should I care? The dirty dog kilt my cousin. A eye for a eye. People need to stop all this marching over nonsense."

"Two wrongs don't make a right," said Ellis Earl. "The police are supposed to arrest people, not kill them. Like the article said, people are marching for fairness. Don't *arrest* white people but *shoot* Negroes. Arrest one the same way you would arrest the other."

Mr. Foster clapped. "Bravo, Mr. Brown! Braaa-vo!"

When the classroom erupted in applause as well, Ellis Earl couldn't believe it. Were they really clapping for something he said? He held in the smile that threatened to spread across his face. He glanced at Philip, expecting his friend to be proud of him. Instead, just as he had on Monday, Philip frowned and looked the other way. Ellis Earl's smile slipped as he wondered what he'd done wrong this time.

Thou Shalt Not Covet

ELLIS EARL DIDN'T QUITE KNOW how to describe the feeling that had stayed with him all morning and straight into lunchtime. Though his class had spent the entire morning analyzing articles from *Jet* magazine, plus other sections of the magazine such as Yesterday in Negro History, Words of the Week, and Weekly Almanac—all this while he was starving!—Ellis Earl didn't mind one bit. Mr. Foster had clapped for him, and that made him feel as if he had accomplished the greatest feat in the world. He was, however, still bothered by Philip's response. So he was annoyed when Philip came and sat next to him during the lunch break.

Ellis Earl was halfway through his delicious lunch of salmon croquets, fried potatoes, and biscuits and halfway through the seventh chapter of *Charlie and the Chocolate Factory* and didn't really want to be bothered at the moment—especially not by someone who was staring at him with an angry expression.

What does Philip have to be mad about? Ellis Earl thought. *He's the one who frowned at me and looked away two times this week.*

Philip glared at Ellis Earl sideways. "I thought you were my friend."

Ellis Earl was taken aback. "I *am* your friend."

"Friends don't try to show up each other all the time," said Philip.

Now Ellis Earl was really confused. He searched his memory. *He* was the one who never knew the answers to Mr. Foster's current events questions. So how could *he* be accused of trying to show up anyone? Ellis Earl's brow furrowed. "Showing you up? How? You know everything."

"Every time *I* give an answer, you always try to come up with a better one. And this time you said the same thing I said, and everybody clapped like you were some hero. You're nothing but a copycat."

"I didn't—" Ellis Earl stopped. He recalled the wave of jealousy that always swept over him when Philip raised his hand in class. He recalled the wave of envy when Philip always answered intelligently. He recalled the feeling of covetousness whenever he wished it were he who knew all the answers and could have intellectual discussions with his teacher. Even though he had participated this last time primarily because he wanted to speak up more in class, he knew that all the times before, he had set out to compete with his friend. But rather than apologizing, Ellis Earl held on to his pride and denied Philip's accusation. "I don't try to show you up. That's just you thinking that you're better than everyone else."

"Stop being so jealous," Philip said.

"I ain't jealous of *you*, Philip Harris," Ellis Earl said, scowling.

The words came out of his mouth, but they were far from his heart. True, Philip was his friend and had been since third grade, but it was also true that Philip lived in town and didn't have to catch a ride to school with the teacher. Philip had a mama and a daddy living under the same roof with him, and he had only three siblings and a grandma living in the house besides that. And from what Philip had told Ellis Earl, their house had six rooms—one of them an indoor toilet even. That was double the number of rooms in Ellis Earl's house with only half the number of people.

Sometimes Philip brought his own lunch. Though the lunch Philip brought from home might sometimes be only a couple of biscuits, those two biscuits were two times more than Ellis Earl had ever brought from home!

With a loud huff, he sank down in his desk and muttered, "You ain't got nothing for me to be jealous about."

Philip stood and narrowed his eyes at Ellis Earl. "Just stop trying to show me up, because you'll never be better than me, Ellis Earl Brown." He stormed back to the other side of the room where he'd been sitting.

Ellis Earl was so bothered by Philip's words that he lost his enthusiasm for his book (but not his lunch; no amount of disdain could cause that). Regardless, Ellis Earl couldn't help but think about the chapter he had just read where the first two golden tickets had been found by spoiled rich children, the first by a boy named Augustus Gloop, and the second by a girl named Veruca Salt. Charlie accused Veruca Salt's father of not playing fair because they were rich and because Mr. Salt had made his workers search for Veruca's golden ticket among the many Wonka bars he had purchased. Charlie's Grandpa Joe had said that no good could ever come from spoiling a child like that.

Charlie's Grandma Josephine had called Augustus Gloop's mother "a revolting woman," while Grandma Georgina had called Augustus himself "a repulsive boy." Ellis Earl wasn't quite sure what those words meant, but he knew that they didn't sound good.

Of Veruca Salt, Grandma Josephine had said that she was even worse than Augustus Gloop. And Grandma Georgina said that Veruca Salt needed a real good spanking. But Ellis Earl knew where Grandma Josephine's and Grandma Georgina's words were coming from. They came from the same place as his competing with Philip. They were jealous that Augustus Gloop and Veruca Salt had found the golden tickets and not Charlie. And the fact that Charlie stood hardly any chance at ever finding a ticket made the jealousy even worse. Ellis Earl knew this because this is how he felt about Philip.

Philip is right. I will never be as good as him, so I might as well stop trying.

Ellis Earl flipped back and forth in his book. He observed the pictures of Augustus Gloop and Veruca Salt. How happy they looked! Ellis Earl thought he wouldn't mind being spoiled for once, even though he felt it was wrong. He had heard Jeannette call Junior's children spoiled often enough. So obviously a child didn't have to live with a rich family to be spoiled.

Ellis Earl closed the book.

His family didn't attend church, but Mama still taught all her children three things: the Twenty-Third Psalm, the Lord's Prayer, and the Ten Commandments. And number ten of those commandments was poking into Ellis Earl's conscience like a prickly cactus:

Thou shalt not covet thy neighbor's house, thou shalt not covet thy neighbor's wife, nor his manservant, nor his maidservant, nor his ox, nor his ass, nor any thing that is thy neighbor's.

Ellis Earl always hesitated when it came to one word in the commandment—the one that meant the same thing as donkey. But some of his siblings got a kick out of saying it because it was the only time Mama allowed them to cuss. Ellis Earl wondered why God would allow a cuss word in his holy book. Mama said God was all-powerful, so he could say whatever he wanted in his own book.

But Mama also cautioned her children about this one commandment more than the others. She said this one sin, *covetousness*, could drive a person to commit any of the others, including idolatry, stealing, lying, and, yes, even killing.

Ellis Earl tried hard to rein in his feelings of jealousy toward Philip. But as he stole glances at him on the other side of the room, the feelings only intensified. Philip even had at least four pairs of pants and four shirts. Ellis Earl only had two of each. And his younger siblings who didn't attend school had only raggedy hand-me-down clothes that were either too big or too small, especially their shoes. Most of them simply went barefoot unless, out of absolute necessity, they had to leave the house.

Ellis Earl couldn't help but wonder if his siblings felt the same about him as he did about Philip.

Not Exactly an African Church

JUST BEFORE THE LUNCH BREAK ENDED, Mr. Foster called Ellis Earl to his desk.

"You look a little distraught, Mr. Brown," he said. "Something troubling you? Anything I can help you with?"

Ellis Earl stuffed his hands in his pockets and shifted his weight from one foot to the other. He wanted to stare at the floor, but he knew that Mr. Foster expected him to make eye contact with him. So that's what he did.

But he wasn't about to tell him about his uncomfortable chat with Philip.

"No, sir," he said to Mr. Foster. "Nothing's bothering me."

"I'm surprised to see you looking so glum," said Mr. Foster. "You should be smiling. You should be proud of yourself after that stellar performance this morning. You did an excellent job with your rebuttal."

Ellis Earl smiled. He figured the word *rebuttal* meant argument, and he liked the way it sounded. Sure, it hurt that Philip had accused him of trying to show him up, but he was still proud of himself. He had done an excellent job with his *rebuttal*! He would be sure to do that the next time Carrie Ann or Jeannette picked a fight with him.

Mr. Foster leaned back in his chair and, with a smile on *his* face, studied Ellis Earl for a moment. "Does your family attend a church, Mr. Brown?" he asked.

The smile immediately disappeared from Ellis Earl's face. "Church?" he asked, as if the question had come from somewhere out of this world as opposed to his teacher right in front of him.

Still smiling, Mr. Foster said, "Yes, church. You know, those little wooden houses of worship, with the steeples on top and the saints inside."

"No, sir, we don't go to church," Ellis Earl answered, still thinking how odd it was of Mr. Foster to ask such a question.

"Easter's this Sunday," said Mr. Foster. "I've asked a few other students to be my guests and participate in our Easter program. I'd like for you to join us. Be a good opportunity for you to practice your speaking skills."

"What's an Easter program?"

"It's not like regular service," said Mr. Foster. "The youth group performs a play and holds a talent show, and the younger children recite speeches. Would you like to do a speech?"

Ellis Earl couldn't control the frown that appeared on his face at the thought of attending church. He didn't mind Mama listening to church music on Sundays, but he didn't want to go to church. His grandparents attended two churches—one on the first and third Sundays of the month, and the other on the second and fourth Sundays of the month. They weren't nice to Ellis Earl's family at all. As a matter of fact, sometimes they could be downright nasty. Even though Mama and all the little ones—Ellis Earl down through Vera—occasionally went to his grandparents' house for Sunday dinner, every bite of food was served up with a generous helping of guilt. His grandparents never failed to remind Mama that God was punishing her for her disobedience toward them when she left home at sixteen to marry Ellis Earl's father. He eventually left the family, just as they had predicted. This, they said, was what *his* father had done to his family. And the apple never falls all that far from the tree.

Ellis Earl, however, knew that his grandparents' assessment of his father, Walter Sr., was terribly unfair. He had not simply up and left his family. He had died.

The man for whom he worked said it happened instantly when lightning struck the tractor he was driving. Still, Ellis Earl's grandparents faulted Mama's disobedience for what the landowner called an act of God. Mama, on the other hand, faulted the landowner, as he was the one who demanded Walter Brown Sr. finish plowing his field, regardless of the approaching thunderstorm.

Ellis Earl wasn't too certain whether he wanted to go to church if other church people were anything like his grandparents. But then again, Mr. Foster obviously attended church, and he didn't appear to be anything like Ellis Earl's grandparents. He was kind and never once when he shared his food made others feel guilty about eating it.

Maybe it wouldn't hurt to give church a try.

"Which church?" Ellis Earl asked before making a commitment. He didn't want to end up at one of the churches where his grandparents attended.

"Emmanuel AME," answered Mr. Foster.

"Is that a Baptist church?"

Mr. Foster eyed him curiously. "No. It's AME: African Methodist Episcopal."

That's a lot of names, thought Ellis Earl. But he said aloud, "Do Baptist people go there?"

"Sometimes," Mr. Foster answered. "Is your family Baptist?"

"Yes," said Ellis Earl. "But I think it's okay for me to go to an African church."

Mr. Foster laughed slightly and said, "It's not exactly an African church, Mr. Brown. It's African Methodist Episcopal, a combination of the Methodist and Episcopal faiths, but *African* distinguishes it from the white Methodist Episcopal Church."

Even more confused, Ellis Earl only nodded.

"And breakfast is served," Mr. Foster added.

At the mention of breakfast, Ellis Earl's mouth watered. "Oh," he said, his mind now made up for sure. "What kind of speech would I have to do?"

Mr. Foster retrieved a large envelope from his desk drawer. "I have a speech that I think would be great for you," he said, removing a sheet of paper from the envelope.

He handed the speech to Ellis Earl.

Ellis Earl studied it. "I have to read this in front of everybody like we do in class?" he asked.

"Well, actually, you have to *recite* it," said Mr. Foster.

"Like memorize it?"

"Yes."

Ellis Earl's eyebrows shot up. "By Sunday?"

"You have four days," said Mr. Foster.

Ellis Earl glanced at the speech. "It's kind of long." He quickly counted the lines. "It's got eighteen lines."

"A few lines a day, Mr. Brown. That's all you need to focus on. Not the whole thing at once."

Ellis Earl didn't say anything.

"You'll have to memorize longer speeches than that if you want to be a lawyer someday," said Mr. Foster. "Plus, if you join us, there might be another opportunity for you to travel someplace special in another couple of weeks or so."

This grabbed Ellis Earl's attention. "Travel? Where?"

Mr. Foster winked. "It's a surprise. For now, let's just say it's someplace *very special* with the chance to meet someone *very important*."

A smile spread across Ellis Earl's face. His heart felt like it skipped a beat or two. He had never traveled anywhere other than to school, his grandparents' house, and his uncle Joseph's house. He didn't want to miss this opportunity. "I'll do my best to memorize the speech," he said eagerly.

"Great," said Mr. Foster. "You sing? We also have a youth choir if you'd like to join."

"No, sir. I don't sing." He thought about his brothers and Jeannette singing their blues. He *would* sing if they allowed him to join them. Maybe if they sang gospel, then they could sing at Mr. Foster's church. But they only sang blues songs, and Ellis Earl knew that wouldn't be appropriate for church. But . . . Mr. Foster *had* said something about a talent show. The school had those sometimes. Each time, Ellis Earl had watched with envy as his classmates sang, danced, and performed one-person plays in front of the entire school. During these talent shows, the performers could sing any kind of song they wished. Some sang church songs, some sang blues, some sang the popular songs that Ellis Earl had heard on the radio. But these talent shows were for schoolchildren only, which the Brown Blues were not.

Maybe if the Brown Blues performed in the talent show at Mr. Foster's church, they could sing any kind of songs they wanted. Maybe it would be a chance for them to actually get heard by someone other than the family. Maybe . . . just maybe . . . it would be an opportunity for them to even get *discovered* by someone important, something they'd long been hoping for.

"Can anybody perform in the talent show?" Ellis Earl asked.

"Of course," said Mr. Foster, a broad smile spreading across his face. "You have a talent you'd like to share?"

"Not me. My—" Ellis Earl hesitated. Mr. Foster's smile was too eager. Too *proud*. Should he tell his teacher about the Brown Blues? It was, after all, *he* that Mr. Foster was inviting to his church to do a speech, not his siblings. He wasn't so sure that he wanted his teacher's attention turned to them instead of him. Besides, they wouldn't even let him sing with them, so why should he do *them* any favors?

"Never mind. I'll just do the speech."

"You sure?"

"Yes, sir. I'm very sure."

"Excellent," said Mr. Foster. "Speak with your mother about permission and let me know tomorrow."

"I will," said Ellis Earl, nodding vigorously. "Thank you for inviting me."

"It's my pleasure, Mr. Brown. I'm looking forward to hearing you recite your speech."

Ellis Earl smiled. But inside he felt something else. Guilt. It was harder to swallow than all the guilt his grandparents ever served with their suppers. He knew he should have asked more about the talent show for his siblings' sake, but oh, how he wanted to keep the spotlight on himself, even if it was only for one day. Now he knew how those two selfish children Augustus Gloop and Veruca Salt felt. Though they already had all they needed, they still wanted that golden ticket. Ellis Earl suddenly felt as greedy as he considered them to be, except his greed was for his teacher's attention.

THURSDAY, MARCH 23

What Bad Luck!

Ellis Earl heard the rain hammering the tin roof before the first drop slipped through the ceiling and plopped on his face.

"Ugh!" he groaned as he wiped his forehead.

He was used to rain coming in through the roof, but it had never happened directly over the mattress where he and Oscar (and now his two nephews) slept.

Ellis Earl shook his brother, who was snoring ever so gently. "Oscar, wake up. We need to move the mattress. Rain coming in right here now."

Oscar moaned and rolled over onto his back. As he did, a drop of rain went *plop* right into his eye.

Groggily repeating Ellis Earl's words, "Rain coming in right here now?" he sat up and eased his spindly legs to the floor.

"You think you can go get a pot from the kitchen while I move the mattress?" asked Ellis Earl.

"I kin."

Can, Ellis Earl thought. But he did not correct his little brother. There were more important matters with which to deal.

What bad luck! he thought. Now they had to find a new place to put the mattress, as there would be no repairs made to their rusty roof. And with the room as small as it was, there were few options. Careful not to wake his nephews, he slid the mattress over just enough so that it was out of the range of the drops of rain.

Oscar returned with two large pots and two mixing bowls, which he and Ellis Earl placed around the room. They knew by heart where the rain dripped in.

Oscar flopped down on the mattress. "I wish we had a different house."

Ellis Earl joined him on the mattress, saying nothing—only listening as the rain hit the pots and bowls.

But after a few moments, Ellis Earl stood abruptly and said, "I just remembered something!"

"What?" Oscar asked, looking confused.

"Hold on." Ellis Earl rushed to the corner of the room to his schoolbooks. Though it was dark in the front room, he was able to find the article clipped from *Jet* magazine. He knew exactly where it was, because he had used it to mark the page in his math book. He returned to the mattress and showed the article to Oscar. "I had to talk about this in class on Monday. I know it's too dark to see, but it says here that the president is working to pass laws for fair housing by 1969."

"What do that mean?" asked Oscar.

"I think it means that the president don't want people living in houses with rusted old tin roofs that leak."

"You think they'll have toilets inside like Uncle Joseph's house?"

"I bet they will!" said Ellis Earl. "And they'll have sinks in the kitchen, too!"

"Won't that be nice!" Oscar said, smiling. He lay back down on the mattress and rested his hands behind his head. "I bet our new house is gonna have paneling on the walls and maybe even rugs on the floor."

"And maybe we'll have a room and not have to sleep in the front room," said Ellis Earl.

"And a bed. We don't need two. I don't mind sharing with you," said Oscar. "No sense in being greedy."

Ellis Earl cringed at the word *greedy*. He thought about how he had refused to tell Mr. Foster about the Brown Blues. How could he think only of himself? Mama had taught them better. He said glumly to Oscar, "It'll just be nice not to have the mattress on the floor anymore."

The boys grew quiet again for a moment before Oscar suddenly blurted out, "Food!"

"What about food?"

"You think the president of the United States is planning on making sure we have some food with these new houses?"

Ellis Earl laughed a little. "Who's gonna put the food in the house, lil' brother? You think the president of the United States is gonna make somebody build some houses *and* put food in them?"

"Yep!" Oscar declared. "A fair house with a icebox full of food!"

"Well, come to think of it," Ellis Earl said, rubbing his chin, "Mr. Foster did say something about a lady lawyer from Mississippi that went to Washington, DC, last week and told them that people down here need food."

Oscar's eyes grew wide. "A *lady* lawyer? Git outta here!"

"It's true," said Ellis Earl. "*And* she's colored."

"Wow," said Oscar, shaking his head. "I can't hardly believe that. Do you know her name?"

"Hmm. I forgot." Ellis Earl scratched his head. "I think it was Mary or something. Oh, yeah. Her name is Miss Mary Ann Wright."

"You think Miss Mary Ann Wright can get us some food?"

Ellis Earl shrugged. "Maybe. Mr. Foster said that there are some programs to help people get food. He said Miss Mary Ann Wright was trying to get those senators to come from Washington, DC, and see that people in Mississippi don't have enough food to eat. I don't know how it works, but maybe she can get them to give us some food."

"Won't that be grand!" Oscar said with a wide grin.

"It sure will be," said Ellis Earl. He hoped Mr.

Foster was right. He hoped the senators would come. But why would they come all the way from Washington, DC, just to see if people in Mississippi were poor or not? The chance of anybody other than Miss Mary Ann Wright caring about poor colored people in Mississippi was as slim as Charlie Bucket finding a golden ticket when he couldn't even buy a candy bar.

When Jeannette entered the room a little while later, Ellis Earl groaned. Why'd she have to get up so soon and spoil his and Oscar's time together?

Jeannette squinted. She couldn't see the pots, but she could hear the pitter-patter of the rain dropping into them. "Good. Y'all already put out pots to catch the rain."

She lit the kerosene lamp. "It's leaking by the mattress now!"

"Uh-huh," Oscar replied.

"Raggedy ol' house," Jeannette said. "Earl, go check the rest of the house, make sho' we ain't got no mo' new leaks."

After a thorough check, Ellis Earl returned to the front room with the glum report that there were indeed two new leaks in the kitchen. This time, Jeannette said a word that she wouldn't dare let

Mama hear her say. And she didn't even bother saying it under her breath as she normally did. Ellis Earl hoped Mama was still asleep and didn't hear it.

He then added fuel to the fire by informing her that they also had run out of pots and bowls. "But I put down a rag," he said quickly, before another colorful word came from Jeannette. "It'll at least soak up the rain."

With a groan, Jeannette stormed over to the window. "Darn yard flooded," she said. "Road, too." She threw up her hands. "Guess ain't nobody going to work today. School neither."

Ellis Earl scurried to the window and peered out. *"Why?"* he moaned, seeing she was right. "Why'd it have to rain so hard?"

He trudged back over to the mattress, plunked himself down, and immediately began to cry.

"You might as well stop that crying," Jeannette said. "You know good and well it ain't gonna change a thing."

Oscar slid an arm around Ellis Earl's shoulders. "It's okay. Missing one day of school ain't gonna hurt you."

Ellis Earl shrugged off Oscar's arm. He jumped up from the mattress. "I don't wanna stay here! I wanna go to school where there's books and food and people learning stuff. I don't wanna be in this leaky old house all day!"

With a tremble in his voice, Oscar said, "I'm here all day."

After seeing the hurt in Oscar's eyes, Ellis Earl regretted his outburst, but he didn't offer an apology. He really *didn't* want to stay in a leaky old house all day. He wanted to go to school.

"What is going on in here?" Mama said. She was still buttoning her flowered housecoat over her nightgown as she entered the front room. "What's all this racket for?"

"Earl being mean to Oscar," Jeannette said. She stared at Ellis Earl as if she wished to throttle him.

"I ain't being mean to nobody," Ellis Earl muttered. "I only said I don't wanna stay in this house all day. I didn't say nothing to Oscar."

"Well, you know Oscar have to stay in this house all day, *every* day," said Jeannette. "So how you think that make him feel when you say stuff like that?"

Ellis Earl wiped tears from his face with the back of his hand. "I didn't mean nothing by it. I just don't wanna miss school."

"Mm-hmm. Sho' you didn't mean nothing," said Jeannette. "You spending too much time wit' that high-class teacher anyways. That's why you act so uppity. Always making fun of the way people talk, like you so proper yo'self."

"We ain't gonna have none of that today, Jeannette," Mama said. "We all got to suffer in this house together if this rain don't let up." She frowned at the rain dripping in through the ceiling. "Lord, I sho' hope Mrs. Chalmers don't fire me 'foe I barely had a chance to git started."

"She oughta understand it if you can't even git to the road, Mama," said Jeannette.

Mama shook her head. "Nah, child. She ain't gon' understand. Not as long as some other colored woman ready and willing to show up in my place just like I was ready and willing to show up in Miss Lucinda's."

"What about the Easter program?" Ellis Earl said, sniffling.

"What about it?" Jeannette asked, sneering. "Ain't like you got no decent clothes to wear to church anyways."

Ellis Earl looked at Mama. "You said I could go.

What if Mr. Foster asks somebody else to do the speech since I won't be there to tell him I can go?"

Mama peered out the window. "It's raining pretty hard out there, Earl. You might not get to go back to school till Monday anyway."

"Monday!" Ellis Earl burst into fresh tears. "No school. No church. No nothing!"

With his outburst, Ellis Earl woke the little nephews. Lil' Walt, the older of the two, announced that he was hungry the minute he opened his eyes.

Mama said to Ellis Earl, "You woke 'em. You feed 'em." She rubbed her temples as if she had a headache, and said with much weariness, "There oughta be some rice still in the icebox from yesterday. Go fix 'em some and bring it in here. Maybe you can read to 'em or something to keep from missing school so much."

Ellis Earl slumped to the kitchen to retrieve the rice. Reading to his nephews would *not* keep him from wishing he was at school. Absolutely nothing could accomplish that feat.

They Are Very Small

WITH ALL THE EXCITEMENT he could muster, Ellis Earl raised his hands high above his head, bugged his eyes, and bared his teeth. He was doing his best to imitate "the wild things."

His nephews, Lil' Walt and Prince, enjoyed the drama even if Ellis Earl didn't. He had borrowed the book *Where the Wild Things Are* from Mr. Foster's library on Tuesday and forgot to return it on Wednesday. Now he was glad he had forgotten. The book was a good way to keep his nephews entertained even though he himself wasn't.

Rain continued to pound the roof, and hunger pangs continued to pound his stomach. A bowl of rice might have been sufficient breakfast for his nephews, but Ellis Earl's stomach begged for more. All he could think of was what kind of lunch he would be missing in Mr. Foster's classroom.

And what if he didn't get to go to the Easter program? More than just the speech, he was desperately looking forward to the breakfast that Mr. Foster said would be served. And what about that special trip? If he couldn't go to the Easter program, then surely Mr. Foster wouldn't ask him to go anyplace else. He hoped the flooded road would dry up by tomorrow and not keep him out of school for another day.

Ellis Earl considered Max, the boy in *Where the Wild Things Are*. As punishment for sassing his mama, Max was sent to his room without supper. But once his adventure was over, his supper was right there waiting for him by his bedside. *And* the supper was still warm. Ellis Earl longed for a warm supper. Actually, he was hungry enough to consider even a cold one, and it was barely seven o'clock in the morning. He shut the book. "All done. Now y'all need to go on back to sleep. It's too early for you little children to be up."

When two-year-old Lil' Walt shook his head

no, Ellis Earl opened the book again. There was no point in trying to get his nephews to lie back down on the mattress where Oscar had already dozed off again. He would read the book one more time, very slowly, in hopes that his nephews would lose interest. But even if they did, Ellis Earl thought, what else was there for them to do?

They couldn't yet read to themselves the way Vera could. They weren't old enough to play checkers or jacks. And they weren't very interested in paper dolls. It would be nice, thought Ellis Earl, if they owned a television like Uncle Joseph. Perhaps something like that would be a good way to keep the little ones entertained when they had nothing else to do. Of course a television would be of no use to them since the house had no electricity.

Ellis Earl released a long, deep sigh. Why did it have to rain so hard? And why did they have to live down a hill where the path flooded? With the path flooded, no one would be able to leave the house. His brothers had tried before—taking off their shoes, rolling up their pant legs, and wading through the water to get to the main road to hitchhike a ride to town. But the results had been nearly disastrous. Some unknown critter lurking in the knee-deep water had bitten Raymond on the foot, causing an infection that lasted for weeks. Since that time, no one else in the family had attempted to wade through the floodwaters.

Ellis Earl turned to the first page of the book and began reading. Lil' Walt pointed to the illustration of Max chasing his dog with a fork and said, "Max bad!"

Ellis Earl studied the picture. Bad or not, he would gladly trade places with Max. Max lived in a house with stairs! But instead of continuing to long for Max's life, he focused on his nephew. "That's right. Max is bad," he said. "Do you remember what happens to Max?"

Lil' Walt cried, "Max git sent to bed without no food and a forest growed in his room!"

"Good job!" said Ellis Earl. "You're remembering the story. You'll be learning to read soon."

Lil' Walt beamed.

After he finished the book, Ellis Earl managed to coax his little nephews to rest a bit on the mattress. "Y'all can get back up when the sun comes out," Ellis Earl told them. He himself sat in the chair next to the kerosene lamp and set about reading his own book, *Charlie and the Chocolate*

Factory. He hadn't gotten far because he kept going back to reread his favorite parts, like the part where Mr. Wonka, the chocolate factory owner, had fired all his workers because some of them were spies. And since he didn't know the spies from the loyal workers, he simply fired everyone. But the big mystery, according to Charlie's Grandpa Joe, was that the factory was still running.

"'We know only one thing about them,'" Ellis Earl read quietly to himself. "'They are very small . . .'"

Ellis Earl closed his eyes and hugged the book to his chest. He imagined himself next to Charlie Bucket as the two of them stood on the street in front of Willy Wonka's chocolate factory, staring at the shadows of tiny people as they busied themselves making candy.

"Who do you think they are?" he would ask Charlie.

Charlie would shrug and say, "I don't know, Ellis Earl. They don't look like people at all to me. Real people aren't that small—only knee-high!"

Then Ellis Earl would say, "They have to be real people. Who else could be in there making that delicious candy?"

Then Charlie would say—

"ELLIS EARL!"

Ellis Earl snapped out of his daydreaming. Charlie Bucket would never yell out his name so rudely. Only Jeannette would do that.

She stalked into the room, snatched the book from his hands, and snapped at him. "I know you ain't in here try'na play like you readin' when all you really doin' is sleepin'."

"I am reading," said Ellis Earl. He grabbed for his book, but Jeannette yanked it back.

"Readin' or sleepin'. I don't care which one you doin'. But I know you better git yo' lil' skinny butt in there and emp' that slop jar."

Ellis Earl rolled his eyes. *Empty. Empty that slop jar*, he thought. But of course he didn't say it. Nor did he want to complete the task. "It's raining," he said.

"So?" Jeannette said, crossing her arms. "I emp' that thing in the rain all the time."

"Not when it's raining *this* hard," Ellis Earl said. He pointed toward the pots and bowls catching the rain leaking through the roof.

Jeannette kicked his foot. "Stop being lazy and git out there to that toilet and emp' that slop jar."

"Can't I at least wait till everybody gets up?" Ellis Earl pleaded.

"It's full. You need to emp' it now."

Ellis Earl huffed and crossed his arms over his chest, too. "Well, it wouldn't be so full if all y'all girls didn't pee so much at night."

Jeannette narrowed her eyes. She held up the copy of *Charlie and the Chocolate Factory*. "Git out there and emp' that slop jar 'foe this lil' book git dumped in it."

With widened eyes and a racing heart, Ellis Earl rushed to the middle room to retrieve the chamber pot before Jeannette could carry out her threat. He wanted to tell Mama, but she was already sound asleep again. Her head was buried deep under the covers, teetering on the edge of the bed she shared with Jewel, Vera, and Beatrice, whose little bodies took up more than their fair share of space.

Ellis Earl could smell the contents of the chamber pot before he even reached it. Jeannette was right; it really did need to be emptied right away. With Mama, all the girls, Oscar, and Lil' Walt having to use it during the night, it probably should have been dumped *during* the night. (Going to the outhouse at night to do his business was the only thing that Ellis Earl had in common with his older brothers. Oscar had been deemed too sickly to go outside in the elements, day or night, to handle his personal business.)

Ellis Earl carefully lifted the stinky white pot by the handle and, very slowly, tiptoed through the kitchen where his brothers slept and out the back door to the outhouse. He couldn't tell tears from rain as both ran heavily down his face. The word *angry* wasn't strong enough to describe how he felt. This time, he really did want to punch Jeannette in the face.

He knew he could have awakened Mama, and the matter would have been settled immediately with Jeannette receiving her just punishment for threatening to dump his book in the chamber pot. Yet he also knew that would only make Jeannette angry enough to retaliate and conjure up something worse to do to him later when Mama wasn't home.

Upon his return from the outhouse, he spotted Lucky, the cat he and Carrie Ann were supposed to have chased away. *Lucky*, he scoffed. He wagged his finger at the cat. "Maybe Carrie Ann was right the first time. Maybe you are bad luck.

We should've used that broom to shoo you on away from here like we were told. Now we're being punished for it. I can't go to school, Mama might lose her job, and I might not get to go to church with Mr. Foster. We should've named you Unlucky."

The cat scooted farther underneath the house until Ellis Earl could see only his eyes. They glowed in the darkness, looking exactly like something that would cause bad luck.

After changing into dry clothes, Ellis Earl hurried back to the front room to retrieve his book. He was disappointed to find Jeannette there waiting for him.

She still had his book.

And she had it open.

"I'm done," said Ellis Earl. "May I have my book back?"

Still looking down and turning a page of *Charlie and the Chocolate Factory*, Jeannette simply said, "Hmmmm."

Ellis Earl dared approach her. He stood right in front of her and extended his hand. "Can I have my book now?"

Still not looking up, Jeannette answered, "I'm reading it."

"But you can't—"

With that Jeannette snapped her head up. With steely eyes, she glared at Ellis Earl. "I *kin* read," she said.

"I—um. I wasn't gonna say that," said Ellis Earl.

"Liar," Jeannette snarled.

Ellis Earl fidgeted. "It's just that—" He searched for the right words. "I've never seen you reading. That's all."

Jeannette narrowed her eyes. "You ain't gotta see somebody reading to know that they read, dummy." She slammed the book shut and tossed it toward Ellis Earl. The book hit the floor.

Jeannette sprang to her feet and leaned toward him. "Jes' 'cause I didn't go past sixth grade, Mr. Smarty Pants, don't mean I can't read that lil' book. I ain't stupid."

Just as Ellis Earl opened his mouth to apologize, Jeannette pushed him so hard that he fell to the floor right beside his book. As Jeannette stalked away, Ellis Earl grabbed his book and hugged it to his chest. He was glad she hadn't given him the opportunity to waste an apology on her.

SATURDAY, MARCH 25

You Clumsy Fool!

THE HANDLE FELT AS IF it would slice straight through his fingers as Ellis Earl carried the heavy bucket of water the thirty steps from the water pump to the washtubs (one for washing, the other for rinsing). The walk wasn't a very long one, but when you had skinny arms like Ellis Earl, and puny muscles that refused to assist you, carrying a bucket of water thirty steps felt about the same as carrying it three hundred steps. Filling up the washtub on Saturday was a chore that Ellis Earl hated more than emptying the chamber pot. At least with the chamber pot it was only one trip to the outhouse and back. But on washday, it felt to Ellis Earl that he made twenty-five trips back and forth from the water pump to the washtub. And today it was only he and Carrie Ann who performed the task.

Ellis Earl had hoped washday would be canceled since Mama had been feeling poorly with a cough and a headache since Thursday afternoon. But washday couldn't be neglected; they had all reworn their few sets of clothing too many times already. They were in desperate need of washing.

Like they did every Saturday, Ellis Earl's older brothers had hitchhiked a ride into town to look for work since the road had cleared from the flooding. Jeannette, who rarely helped tote water anyway, was inside helping with the multitude of little children. Oscar, of course, was ill. And Beatrice and Deidra had suddenly come down with coughs, which Ellis Earl didn't believe was even a tiny bit true, seeing they had only started coughing when Mama announced that the tubs had to be filled. But it was not his job to convince Mama otherwise. So that left only him and Carrie Ann to complete a job usually done by five.

At least the weather was springlike, and warm enough that only a T-shirt was required and not long sleeves. Hauling water was a harrowing job made worse when the weather was cold. Plus, it was nice to see the sun bright and shiny after Thursday's dismal weather. Friday hadn't been bad. The sun had come out, but the road was still in no condition for even walking on until late evening. The family figured that Mama had probably lost her temporary job with Mrs. Chalmers by now, but the truth would be confirmed by the brothers after they had ventured into town today.

As he trudged along—water sloshing out of the bucket, wetting his clothes—Ellis Earl thought about three things:

One: how rotten it was that he didn't get to go to school for two days because of the rain.

Two: how rotten it was that he wouldn't get to go to church with Mr. Foster because he didn't get to go to school *because of the rain*.

Three: something that had Ellis Earl ruffled even though it shouldn't have—whether Charlie Bucket would find a golden ticket.

He was just as sad as Charlie when Charlie did not find a golden ticket wrapped around the chocolate bar he got for his birthday. Of course Ellis Earl knew that Charlie probably wouldn't find a ticket then, because that would have been too easy and the book probably wouldn't have been as much fun to read. He knew that Charlie *had* to be one of the children to find a ticket because the book was called *Charlie and the Chocolate Factory*. Surely Charlie wasn't just going to stand outside the factory forever, staring at the shadows of the knee-high people working inside.

Ellis Earl got to thinking. He pondered how strange it was that Charlie *happened* to get a candy bar on his birthday, that his birthday *happened* to fall on the week after Willy Wonka *happened* to announce his contest. He liked the idea of things falling perfectly into place for Charlie, as he felt sure they would. He made a mental note that if he ever *happened* to write a book, he would make sure that everything fell perfectly into place for the boy he would write about, too.

Then he *really* got to thinking. How delightful it would be if he were a character in a book and the author made everything fall perfectly into place for him! Ellis Earl grinned at the thought.

So caught up in his thoughts about Charlie Bucket, Ellis Earl neglected to notice that Carrie Ann had stopped right in front of the big washtub.

When he rammed into her, she flipped over into the tub, which was half full of water, her full bucket spilling onto the ground.

"Ellis Earl! You clumsy fool!" Carrie Ann cried. "How come you can't watch where you goin'!"

Ellis Earl quickly placed his bucket on the ground. "I'm so sorry, Carrie Ann," he said, reaching out to help her up. "I didn't mean to. I didn't see you."

"You need to stop daydreaming so much!" Carrie Ann cried. "You coulda drowned me!"

"You can't drown in that little water. You can't do nothing but get wet."

Carrie Ann swiped at Ellis Earl's hand, trying to push it away. "I kin get myself out." She grabbed the sides of the tin tub and hoisted herself out.

"I said I was sorry," Ellis Earl muttered.

"Well, sorry ain't gonna dry my clothes, *is it*, Ellis Earl Brown?" Carrie Ann stormed over and retrieved her bucket from the other side of the tub. She thrust it toward Ellis Earl's face. "After you finish pouring your bucket in, you might as well git ready to use both of them skinny arms 'cause you 'bout to fill up this for me."

"I said I was sorry," mumbled Ellis Earl a third

time. He poured the water from his bucket into the washtub. Without complaint, he took the other bucket from Carrie Ann and headed back to the pump. As he trekked along the well-worn path, he was still thinking about Charlie Bucket, and how lucky he was that he didn't have a cantankerous little sister to contend with.

"Ellis EARL!" the bitter yell came from the back door of the house. "What did you do to Carrie Ann?"

Jeannette's voice halted Ellis Earl's steps. *Correction,* he thought, as his back stiffened. *Charlie is lucky he doesn't have a cranky* older *sister to deal with.*

Where There's a Will

After a thorough scolding from Jeannette, Ellis Earl crossed his arms and huffed. Carrie Ann not only had accused him of intentionally pushing her into the tub; she also had told Jeannette that they had kept Lucky. "It was all Earl's idea," Carrie Ann had tattled.

Traitor! thought Ellis Earl, clenching his teeth. *She promised she wouldn't tell!*

He'd known Jeannette would eventually learn Lucky was still there, but he could have at least claimed that the cat had returned on his own accord—not that they had refused to shoo him away as they'd been told.

Ellis Earl unfolded his arms, stopped his huffing, and returned to filling the washtubs. He knew that Carrie Ann was only pretending to be traumatized so that she wouldn't have to work.

He wished he could do the same. With all the work he did around the house, he barely had time for reading before the kerosene lamp was turned off at night. When he wasn't having to help care for the little children, he was having to clean up after them, even if it was just wiping up spilled water from the floor. But there were other things, too, like yesterday, when it was his and Carrie Ann's turn to do the dishes. That task seemed to take forever. First water had to be pumped from the well to fill both the dishwashing pan and the rinse pan. Then the dishwashing water had to be heated on the stove. The dishes had to be washed, rinsed, dried, *and* put away. Such a daunting chore after fifteen people had eaten!

Oh, what Ellis Earl wouldn't have given to be inside the house at that moment, relaxing on a comfortable chair (if they had one), reading his book—with Lucky curled up on his lap, content and softly purring.

Oh, what he wouldn't give to live in a nice

house—a real house—with a fireplace or something like that. A house with a big window, with real curtains—thick curtains—so the cold couldn't come through in the wintertime and make Oscar cough, and the heat of the sun couldn't come through in the summertime and make everyone feel as though they would suffocate.

Oh, what he wouldn't give to live in a house with a rug on the floor, like the thick green one Uncle Joseph had in his house. And a big couch in the front room! A big, soft brown couch like Uncle Joseph's couch. And the short couch that Uncle Joseph called a love seat and the chair that he called a "lazy boy." And the wooden table in the center of all of it. And the two tables on each end of the couch. And most of all, oh, what he wouldn't give to have that television that Uncle Joseph and his family watched at night.

But Ellis Earl knew there was no sense in daydreaming about a life he would never have. His wishing was about as hopeless as Charlie Bucket's, who had to walk past Mr. Willy Wonka's factory twice a day, sniffing the sensational scent of delicious chocolate he could never eat.

So lost in his thoughts again, he almost missed

the sound of a car approaching the front of the house. He recognized the sound of that car even if he only heard it rumbling at the end of the path waiting for him and Carrie Ann to join the carpoolers heading to school each morning. Ellis Earl didn't know whether to smile or worry that Mr. Foster had come to his house on a Saturday morning. But the one thing that he was absolutely sure of was that he'd better rush to that car and see what Mr. Foster wanted before he had a chance to get out and come *inside* the house. Ellis Earl just knew he'd die from embarrassment if he did.

Before Mr. Foster killed the engine of his station wagon, Ellis Earl had raced around the house and sprinted toward the driver's side door. "Hey, Mr. Foster!" he said, waving feverishly. "What you doing here?"

Mr. Foster, sticking his hand out the window and waving, replied, "Morning, Mr. Brown. I've missed you these last two days."

"Our road flooded," answered Ellis Earl.

Mr. Foster nodded. "I know. Just wanted to acknowledge that you were missed."

"You came all the way to my house to tell me that?" Ellis Earl asked. He glanced toward the front door of the house, hoping none of his family would come out.

"I came to speak with your mother, actually," said Mr. Foster.

"She ain't—I mean—she's not feeling too good," said Ellis Earl. "She might have a cold. You need me to tell her something?"

"Did you ask her about the Easter program?"

"Yes, sir. She said I could go. But then I didn't get to go to school, so she didn't know if you were still gonna take me or not."

"Of course," said Mr. Foster, smiling. "You got that speech memorized?"

Ellis Earl's heart felt like it fell into his stomach. Since he'd thought there was no way he would possibly get to go to the Easter program, he hadn't bothered with the speech! He spent what little free time he had reading *Charlie and the Chocolate Factory* instead. He placed his hands behind his back and crossed his fingers. "I've been practicing," he said.

"Care to share a bit with me?"

Ellis Earl tried to swallow down his nervousness. Yet he still felt the familiar trickle of sweat suddenly roll from his armpits and down his sides. "Um, I don't want to spoil it for you," he said. "So I'll just save it for tomorrow. What time you picking me up?"

"Around eight. Breakfast starts at nine. I have a few other students to pick up after you, so that gives me plenty of time."

With it being washday, Ellis Earl realized he faced another dilemma. His "good" clothes would be washed today, and they probably wouldn't be dry by morning. He could always just take them out of the pile of dirty clothes, but he knew Mama would never go for that. *Maybe I just shouldn't go*, thought Ellis Earl. But then he thought about the breakfast. There was no way he would miss that.

"Something wrong, Mr. Brown?" asked Mr. Foster. "You look like you've just received bad news."

"I—" Ellis Earl began. He so badly wanted to go to the Easter program—not just for the food, but also because Mr. Foster said he would be picking up other students. With the food, the speeches, and his classmates, going to church would almost be like going to school, except he wouldn't have to take any tests.

Just tell the truth, boy! Ellis Earl heard a voice shout in his mind. The voice sounded a lot like Uncle Joseph's when Ellis Earl had broken a plate at his house once and was afraid he would get in trouble for it. That time, too, he had crossed his fingers behind his back and lied to Uncle Joseph, blaming the broken plate on one of the younger children. Uncle Joseph's sternness had convinced him to confess.

Ellis Earl took a deep breath and relaxed his hands to his sides. "I don't have anything to wear to church," he said. When Mr. Foster frowned, Ellis Earl felt even worse. "I'm sorry," he said. "I guess I can't go to church tomorrow."

"What do you mean you don't have anything to wear?" asked Mr. Foster. "What's wrong with the clothes you wear to school? Church is a place where you are free to come as you are. No one is expecting you to wear something fancy."

"Oh, I didn't mean I couldn't wear my school clothes," Ellis Earl said quickly. "It's just that today is washday, and my clothes won't be dry by tomorrow."

The frown on Mr. Foster's face softened. "That

won't be a problem, Mr. Brown. Where there's a will, there's a way."

"Sir?"

"Don't worry about what you'll wear tomorrow," said Mr. Foster. "Just memorize that speech. I'll take care of the rest."

SUNDAY, MARCH 26

You Gon' Be Somebody

"PLEASE DON'T TURN ON THE RADIO this morning," Ellis Earl begged Mama.

Mama sat on the edge of the chair as she helped Ellis Earl try to figure out how to wear the tie Mr. Foster had bought him. The tie, along with the rest of the clothes befitting a church boy, were brand-new and fit Ellis Earl perfectly. But since neither he nor his mama had ever tied a necktie, they had a hard time making it look right.

Frustrated, Mama slipped the tie from around Ellis Earl's collar and placed it in his hands. "You just gotta wait for yo' teacher to get here. Don't know why he said you didn't need fancy clothes to go to church, then turn right 'round and *buy* you some fancy clothes."

"He said he just felt like doing something special for me," said Ellis Earl.

Mama relaxed and changed her tone. "I'm glad he did. You look real nice, son. Wit' or wit'out the necktie."

When a smile spread across Ellis Earl's face, Mama asked, "Can I turn on my radio now? I'll keep it down real low."

Ellis Earl shook his head. "I like the quiet. And I like it when ain't nobody up but me and you."

"I'm happy to spend time wit' you, too, but the rest of 'em be up directly—soon as them lil' children start stirring 'round, keeping up a racket."

Ellis Earl stared down at the mattress where his brother and nephews slept soundly. "I hope Mr. Foster gets here before any of 'em wake up. I don't want 'em to wake up Carrie Ann. I don't want her to start all that crying again."

"I feel bad that she can't go. But Carr'Ann know she ain't got nothin' decent to wear to church."

"But Mr. Foster said—"

Mama cut him off. "I know what he said. But what did he *do*?"

"He just wanted me to look extra nice, Mama."

"Baby, yo' teacher know it ain't right to come to church looking any ol' kinda way."

Ellis Earl considered this. "Maybe next time I'll ask Mr. Foster if he can get Carrie Ann a dress and some shoes."

Mama gave Ellis Earl a stern look. "Boy, don't you go askin' yo' teacher for no clothes."

Ellis Earl rubbed his hand along the crease in his pants. "But he gave me some clothes, and you didn't say nothing."

"If he *give 'em* to you, that's fine," said Mama, her tone firm. "We accept charity, but we don't beg nobody for it. So don't you go embarrassing yo'self by askin' nobody for nothin'. You hear me?"

Ellis Earl's shoulders slumped. "Yes, ma'am," he said quietly.

As he sat in the other chair, Ellis Earl folded the tie meticulously and held it in his hand, staring at the shiny navy and white stripes. The navy matched his slacks, and the white matched his shirt. Just as she did daily with the old dresses she wore into town, Mama had starched and ironed Ellis Earl's new shirt. He liked how it smelled crispy clean. Mr. Foster had brought him the clothes the previous evening, calling it an Easter gift. Ellis Earl wasn't sure if people really gave gifts on Easter, but he sure was happy Mr. Foster gave him one.

His brothers had made fun of him, calling him his teacher's pet. He was glad they were still asleep; he didn't need to hear them tease him more, and he was sure they would think he looked ridiculous all dressed up the way he was.

"Yo' teacher coming all the way to the house again, ain't he?" Mama asked.

"Yes, ma'am," replied Ellis Earl.

"Good. 'Cause you don't need to be walking all the way up the path by yo'self this morning."

"I did it before," said Ellis Earl. "That one time Carrie Ann was sick."

"This different," said Mama. "This Sunday. Ain't too many peoples goin' 'bout the roads this morning to spot you if something happen. Besides, I don't know why you act like the teacher can't come all the way to the house every day. It ain't like he ain't ever seen it before."

I don't want everybody else seeing it, Ellis Earl wanted to say. But he knew it would hurt his mama's feelings, so he kept his thoughts to himself. He wasn't too eager to walk down a dusty road in such fancy clothes anyway, especially seeing that Mama had shined his shoes with Vaseline.

"Stand up and let me have a good look at you," said Mama.

When Ellis Earl stood before her, Eloise Brown smiled. "You gon' be a fine young man, Ellis Earl Brown. You gon' be somebody one day."

"Thank you, Mama," Ellis Earl said.

Mama stretched out her hands. "Give me a hug."

"You feel kind of warm, Mama," Ellis Earl said after he hugged her. "You still feeling sick?"

"I'm okay," Mama said, still smiling. "Headache's gone. Coughing done calmed down. Just warm 'cause it's a lil' warm in here."

Ellis Earl sat back down and looked over at Oscar. "You think Oscar will get better before his birthday?"

"The weather warming up," Mama said quietly. "He'll get better. It's the cold that made him sick. The warmth will make him well."

"It was warm yesterday, and both of y'all were sick."

"I'm better," Mama said, nodding. "In due time, Oscar will get better, too."

"You think a prayer will work?"

"A prayer never hurt," said Mama.

"I'll say a prayer for him since I'm going to church."

Mama smiled. "You don't have to go to church to say a prayer, baby."

"I know," Ellis Earl said. He fiddled with the tie. "It just feels right though."

"Then you do what feels right."

"How come we don't go to church?"

"Look at how you dressed, baby."

Ellis Earl glanced down at his clothes.

"Ain't none of us got them kinda clothes for church," Mama said. "I ain't had a nice dress to wear in near 'bout twenty years. Shoes neither. Had too many babies to still fit the good clothes I *did* have when I left home. So how I'm supposed to get enough good clothes for *all* my children to go to church?"

"Mr. Foster said—"

Mama cut Ellis Earl off with a look. "Church ain't no place for raggedy ol' clothes. A person oughta come before the Lord with some respectability."

"Ain't we before the Lord all the time? You said God is everywhere. So how come we have to dress up on Sunday when we go to a church building?"

"'Cause that's just the way it is, Earl. Always was. Always will be. I didn't make the rules. And I sho' ain't 'bout to change 'em by showing up at church in no raggedy, faded dress and no dusty, wore-out shoes."

"I'm sorry, Mama," said Ellis Earl.

Mama stared down at her hands. "It's okay, baby. I didn't mean to answer you so rough." For a moment, Ellis Earl thought she might cry. Instead she smiled and said, "Just thinking about when I used to sing in the choir. Could sing real good, too. I sung a few solos in my day."

She leaned back in her chair, closed her eyes, and said, "I sung right on up till y'all's daddy showed up. That's when I stopped going to church."

Ellis Earl didn't ask questions. He had heard the story many times before. Whenever Mama got lost in her Sunday morning gospel singing, she would tell her children about how she used to sing in the choir, and about how their daddy showed up one Sunday morning and swept her off her feet. She was sixteen. He was eighteen. Two weeks later, they were husband and wife. Because of her parents' disapproval, she hadn't been to church since.

"One day, when I'm a lawyer and a teacher and a book writer, I'm gonna buy you a dress," said Ellis Earl. "A real pretty one. And some shoes."

"And I'm gon' wear that dress and them shoes real proud," said Mama. "I know it gon' happen, too. 'Cause one day you gon' make something of yo'self, Ellis Earl Brown. Mark my words. You gon' be somebody one day. I don't know if you gon' be all them things at once, but I believe you kin be anything you want to be."

"I think I can be all those things at once," Ellis Earl said, straightening his shoulders. "Look how fast I memorized that speech."

"That you did," Mama said.

"And I only needed help with one word. *Messiah*. I didn't know that's what Jesus was called."

"Well, that's my fault. Least I could do is have a Bible in the house if I ain't gon' take my children to church."

Ellis Earl reached over and took his mama's hand. "Even without a Bible, you still taught us the Lord's Prayer, and the Twenty-Third Psalm, and the Ten Commandments."

"Humph," said Mama, smiling. "I did, didn't I?"

"And don't worry. One day we're gonna have all those things. A Bible. A good house. Good clothes. And a lot of food."

Mama's smile got brighter. "Yo' daddy wanted to name you Hope," she said. "After his great-granddaddy. But I told him Hope didn't sound right to me for a person's name. Hope is something a person have, not what they named. Maybe I should've listened to him. He musta knowed you'd be a child full of hope."

So. Much. Food.

With church being a wholly new experience for him, Ellis Earl's palms sweated as he awaited Mr. Foster's arrival. He stood on the porch and watched the road—peering beyond the trees—occasionally glancing down at the speech in his hand, just in case.

Even though Mama had told him how to pronounce it, he was still unsure about that word *Messiah*. From its spelling, Ellis Earl pronounced it "Mess-EE-ah" since Jesus came with a message from heaven. But Mama told him the proper pronunciation was "Mus-EYE-ah." Ellis Earl wondered whether she remembered the correct pronunciation, seeing she hadn't been to church in over twenty years. He thought maybe he should go with his pronunciation instead.

When he finally spotted the lime-green station wagon coming slowly down the road, his heart beat so fast that he thought it might race right out of his chest. He took deep breaths and muttered to himself to calm down.

But calm down he didn't, especially when Lucky leapt up on the porch and began rubbing against his pant leg.

Ellis Earl tried to shoo him away. "Get back under the house, Lucky!"

"Meow," Lucky said gently. He gazed at Ellis Earl, demanding his attention.

"Not now, Lucky," Ellis Earl said. "I'm going to church. You getting my new clothes dirty. I'll play later." He figured he could, now that Jeannette knew their secret and didn't seem to care that they'd kept Lucky.

When Lucky refused to budge, Ellis Earl gently nudged him with a little kick.

Lucky hissed and scratched at Ellis Earl, leaving a mark on his shiny black shoe just as Mr. Foster's car pulled in front of the house. Lucky dashed off the porch and back underneath the house.

By now, not only were Ellis Earl's palms sweating, but his armpits, too—and he had the stains on his brand-new white shirt to prove it.

By the time Ellis Earl reached the car, he was totally flustered. It didn't help any that Philip was apparently one of the other children whom Mr. Foster had also invited to the Easter program *and* he had picked him up before he picked up Ellis Earl. Though Mr. Foster had seen his house before, Philip had not. Ellis Earl wished he could dash underneath the house and join Lucky.

Instead he climbed into the back seat, uttered "Good morning," and stared down at his speech. He hated the look that he thought he saw on Philip's face as he gaped at the house—a look that said, *What a dump!*

By the time Mr. Foster picked up three other boys—Dale Harper, Jerry Jones, and Willie Greene—Ellis Earl hoped that Philip had forgotten what his house looked like. In Ellis Earl's opinion, they had stopped at three other "dumps" that looked no better than the one in which he lived.

Even so, the other boys, including Philip, also

had fancy clothes that Ellis Earl had never seen them wear to school. He wondered if Mr. Foster had given them all Easter gifts or if the other boys just happened to have fancy church clothes already. He didn't ask, of course. He was just happy to fit in.

Though he had never been to church, except for funerals, as soon as he stepped inside the front door, Ellis Earl felt a familiarity with the place. Perhaps, he thought, it was because inside the room that Mr. Foster had called the banquet hall, Ellis Earl saw several more of his classmates and other students he recognized from school. But more importantly, he saw food. Lots of food. Biscuits. Bacon. Eggs. Fried potatoes. Grits. Sausage. All laid out on two long tables near the entrance of the room.

Ellis Earl suddenly felt horrible. He wished his siblings were with him, especially Oscar and Carrie Ann. He imagined how wonderful it would have been for all of them to enjoy this abundance of food, then afterward recite speeches. As he took in the crowd, he noticed there were children who looked as young as his niece Vera. *Vera would love to be here*, he thought. *I bet she could remember a speech.*

Though Ellis Earl felt sorrow over the absence of his siblings, the presence of his classmates and the abundance of food made him feel better. Plus, he felt that there was more—something that said he belonged at Emmanuel African Methodist Episcopal Church. He allowed his shoulders to relax as Mr. Foster led them to the table where his other classmates sat.

Ellis Earl was surprised to see the faces of his classmates light up as he approached the table. "Y'all look so *gooood*," said his usually shy classmate Cora Scott. This surprised Ellis Earl. Cora rarely spoke to anyone at school, and she certainly never spoke to him. She sat at the middle desk, in the first row of the classroom, directly in front of Mr. Foster's desk. She was very smart, Ellis Earl knew, because Mr. Foster always praised her for getting excellent marks on her tests. Yet she rarely raised her hand when Mr. Foster encouraged class participation. She spoke only when she was assigned, such as during current events presentations.

Ellis Earl wondered whether Cora didn't talk much, not because she was shy, but because she was often teased by some of the other girls in the class. And this teasing was due to the fact that

Cora looked like no one else in the school except her two younger brothers—one in third grade like Carrie Ann and the other in fourth.

Cora and both her brothers looked white. They even had freckles and red hair, except their hair was fuzzy like other colored people's hair rather than smooth like the hair of the few white people whom Ellis Earl had seen in his lifetime, like some of the teachers at his school.

Cora also spoke differently than most of the students in their class. She spoke "proper," as the other girls often teased.

She waved them over. "Philip and Ellis Earl, come sit by me."

This, too, surprised Ellis Earl. He had no idea Cora even took notice of him. Stuffing his hands in his pockets, he tried to hide the nervousness that suddenly overtook him as he followed Philip to the table where Cora was sitting.

After a few minutes, all the tables in the banquet hall were full with both children and adults. Ellis Earl's heart, as well, was full. When he should have been nervous in this unfamiliar place, he felt welcome and warm. For a moment he forgot about his troubles at home as he glanced around the room at the smiling faces and people greeting and hugging one another.

The mouthwatering aroma of buttered biscuits and bacon only added to his joy. After a blessing of the meal, the elderly and the adults assisting young children were instructed to line up and fix their plates. Ellis Earl did a mental count of the number of people already in line, and he began to fear what he always feared at home: *What if there isn't enough food to feed everyone?* The rumbling of his empty stomach magnified this fear.

But his anxiety was short-lived. For as soon as that group had gone through the line and received hearty helpings from the buffet table, ladies in white dresses, white shoes, and white hair bonnets brought more food from another room.

Ellis Earl nearly cried from delight. So. Much. Food.

Finally it was time for his table to form a line. Ellis Earl's heart thumped with joy. His eyes grew round, and his mouth literally watered as he approached the table. The only time he ever ate bacon and sausage was at his grandparents' house, and even then it was left over from their own earlier breakfast—never fresh. This meat, however, was so fresh from the skillet that it was still shiny. And the biscuits—oh, how they glistened with butter!

With an eager nod, Ellis Earl accepted every food item presented to him: crispy bacon, flaky biscuits, fried potatoes, buttery grits, fluffy eggs, scrumptious sausage, and orange juice—something that Ellis Earl definitely never had at home! The food was so delicious that Ellis Earl seemed to drink it rather than eat it. While his classmates chatted as they ate, Ellis Earl never once looked up from his plate. He was the first at his table to finish. He had eaten so fast that there were still people in line waiting to be served. He looked around the table, regretting that he had gobbled down his food so fast. His classmates still had almost-full plates.

Ellis Earl tried not to lament over his empty plate but instead to concentrate on his speech. Although he had it memorized, he thought it might be wise to take another peek at it just the same. But when he reached into his pocket, it wasn't there!

He tried the other pocket.

Empty.

Had it fallen out in Mr. Foster's car?

I know it, he reassured himself. *I don't need to look at it again.*

Yet every time he tried to conjure the words from his memory, all he saw was white space and that one word that he wasn't sure how to pronounce: *Messiah.*

So he tried to form words around it.

The Messiah has come.

No.

The Messiah is here.

No.

The Messiah has risen.

Yes!

Risen. Because it's Easter. So the Messiah has risen.

Ellis Earl repeated the words, yet they were still the only words that he could remember, regardless of how hard he concentrated.

Ellis Earl jumped when Cora tapped him on the shoulder.

"You okay?" she asked.

"Um, yes," said Ellis Earl. "I'm fine."

With a worried look, Cora handed him her napkin. "You're sweating. And you're talking to yourself."

Ellis Earl took the napkin and wiped sweat from his forehead. He couldn't understand why his mind was blank. This had never happened to him before. He felt as if he might throw up—something he certainly didn't want to do. He didn't want to return home with an empty stomach after having just filled it with such delicious food.

"I can't remember my speech," he told Cora.

She shrugged. "You've got plenty of time to study it. All the little children have to go first." She leaned toward Ellis Earl and whispered, "And none of them *ever* remember their speeches. Some of them even cry."

"Um, thanks," said Ellis Earl, feeling even more insecure about the speech.

Cora glanced at his empty plate. "You eat fast," she said.

Ellis Earl replied with a half-hearted smile, but in his mind he was asking Cora whether she planned to finish the scattering of food left on her plate: two strips of bacon, a few forks of eggs, and a biscuit. Plus, she still had half of her orange juice remaining in her cup. Ellis Earl dismissed the thought from his head and instead asked Cora if she always attended church.

"Every Sunday," she replied with disdain. "And Wednesday, for Bible study. And Thursday, for choir practice. And Saturday, for Bible training."

"That's a lotta church," replied Ellis Earl. Then he winced when he realized he had combined the words *lot* and *of* into *lotta*. He reminded himself to be more proper with his speech around Cora.

Cora picked up her biscuit and took a gingerly bite. "My daddy's a deacon," she said matter-of-factly. "We never miss church."

"Oh," Ellis Earl replied. It took every ounce of his willpower not to drool as Cora picked up a crispy strip of bacon and took her time nibbling it.

"Where do you normally go to church?" she asked. "Morning Star or Eastern Star?"

"I don't go to either one." Those were the two churches of which his grandparents were members. The same preacher pastored both churches.

"You're COGIC?" asked Cora, her brows raised.

"What's COGIC?" asked Ellis Earl.

Cora giggled and said, "Obviously not, since you don't even know what it is. COGIC stands for the first letters in the name Church of God in Christ. I should've known you weren't COGIC. You probably wouldn't be here at Emmanuel if you were. I don't think COGIC people go to other churches."

With a shrug, Ellis Earl said, "I don't know anything about all that."

Cora looked confused. "So if you're not AME, and you're not Baptist or COGIC, then what *are* you?" She squinted at him. "You're not Catholic or Presbyterian, are you?"

Curious, Ellis Earl asked, "What if I am?"

Cora picked up a forkful of eggs, pointed it at him, and asked, "You go to church with white folks?"

Ellis Earl frowned. "Of course not."

"Then you're not Catholic or Presbyterian," said Cora, and she popped the eggs into her mouth. "Colored folks don't have a Catholic or Presbyterian church around here. As a matter of fact, I've never even heard of a colored Presbyterian."

"I don't understand anything you're saying," said Ellis Earl.

"Well," said Cora, munching on the eggs and talking at the same time, "there are only four colored churches around here. Ours, Emmanuel AME; the two Baptist churches, Morning Star and Eastern Star; and the COGIC church, Greater Zion. So if you're not a member of one of them, then you either go to church with white folks or you don't go at all."

"I don't go at all," Ellis Earl said quietly.

Cora's eyes bugged. "You're an atheist?"

"What's that?"

"That means you don't believe in God."

"If I didn't believe in God, I wouldn't be at church."

"Not everybody who goes to church believes in God," said Cora. "Some folks go because it makes them feel good. Some go to impress other people. And some go because somebody else *makes* them go. And some go just in case."

"Just in case what?"

"Just in case there really is a God," answered Cora, "and they don't want to end up in hell."

"Oh," said Ellis Earl. "I believe in God. But my family doesn't go to church."

"That's too bad," said Cora. She picked up her last strip of bacon and offered it to Ellis Earl.

"No, thanks," he said. Surprisingly, he had lost his appetite. All that talk about churches and belief in God had him too confused to care for food. His grandparents attended two churches, and they weren't the nicest of people. Cora had sounded disgruntled herself when she noted her weekly church attendance. So why was it too bad that his family didn't attend at all?

He didn't have long to ponder, as a man he assumed to be Cora's father—a man with freckled, light brown skin and a bushy red Afro—entered the banquet hall and announced that the Easter program would begin in ten minutes.

As they stood to exit the banquet hall, Ellis Earl noticed a slip of paper near his chair. "My speech!" he said.

Since he was still unsure whose pronunciation of the word *Messiah* was correct, his or Mama's, he decided to ask Cora.

"Mus-EYE-ah," she said, pronouncing the word as Mama had.

Ellis Earl smiled. He felt a warmth envelop him when Cora said the word in her beautiful voice. "Thank you," he said. "And Cora?"

"Yes?"

"Don't listen to those girls in class," said Ellis Earl. "You should speak up more. You have important things to say."

Cora smiled. "Thank you, Ellis Earl."

Carry the Good News to Your Brothers

THE PLACE WHERE CORA led Ellis Earl and their classmates was called a sanctuary. Though Ellis Earl had never looked up the word in the big Merriam-Webster's dictionary that Mr. Foster kept on his desk, he knew what it meant.

"Safety," he whispered to himself as he scooted on to a pew toward the front of the sunlit room.

Philip, who was right behind him, whispered back, "What?"

"Nothing," said Ellis Earl. "Just talking to myself."

Philip shrugged and sat down.

Ellis Earl leaned toward Cora. "I like this place," he whispered. "You have a nice church." The only other church he had seen was the one where his father's and his sister Eloise's funerals had been held. That church was tiny and didn't have a room called a banquet hall like Cora's church. It only had one room, and it was entered as soon as one walked through the front door. This church also had shiny wood pews and shiny wood floors. The windows had patterns of many colors, which made the sun display glimmering lights throughout the room.

"We had those put in last Easter," Cora whispered.

"Huh?"

"The stained glass windows." Cora pointed toward a window. "You were staring at them."

"They're beautiful," said Ellis Earl. "Everything is."

When a tiny woman with a huge, perfectly round Afro entered the sanctuary and strolled to the piano, Cora nudged Ellis Earl. "That's my mama. The program's about to start."

All the safety that Ellis Earl had felt when he first stepped into the sanctuary suddenly disappeared. Butterflies replaced it. They fluttered in his stomach.

He took a deep breath, closed his eyes, and reassured himself that he was ready to recite a speech in front of all these people. If children as small as his niece Vera could do it, then so could he.

Cora's mother played beautifully. Ellis Earl recognized the song. He had heard it on the radio when Mama listened to her church music on Sunday mornings.

He wasn't familiar with all the lyrics, but he was happy to be able to sing along with the chorus, for that he knew by heart:

We're marching to Zion,
Beautiful, beautiful Zion.
We're marching upward to Zion,
The beautiful city of God.

Ellis Earl didn't love many of the songs he heard on the radio, but this one he did. Some of the others, instead of sweet melodies, sounded more like a bunch of screaming. This song was "hummable," as Mama liked to say. Humming her church songs was one of her favorite things to do. Ellis Earl opened his eyes and watched all the mamas in the room. Some sat with their children, their arms draped around them. How Ellis Earl longed for this. He wished there were a way to get his whole family to church. His older brothers didn't care much for Mama's church music on the radio, but perhaps they would feel differently in this place. This beautiful place with the sun streaming through its stained glass windows. Ellis Earl again felt guilty for not mentioning the Brown Blues to Mr. Foster. Maybe they could have participated in the talent show. Maybe they even could have won. Maybe that could have been the ticket to getting the whole family to church . . .

Once the program officially started and the children had begun their speeches, Ellis Earl was confident that his performance would be stellar, just like in class with his rebuttal. When it was his turn, he proudly strode to the front of the sanctuary and stood on the stool behind the podium. He cleared his throat and announced his name and the title of his speech: "The Grave Could Not Keep Him."

The grave could not keep Him;
The Messiah had risen.
Mary and Joanna searched,
But their Lord could not be found.
A man in white,
An Angel, they say,
Announced from the empty tomb,
"Why are you looking
For the Living among the dead?
The Lord is not here;
He has risen
Just as He said."
"What joy!" announced Mary.
"We must tell the others."
"Yes, hurry!" said the Angel.
"Carry the good news to your brothers."
The grave could not keep Him;
The Messiah had risen.

After his speech and the applause that followed, Ellis Earl could not contain his joy. Like the women at the tomb, he wanted to share this experience. He wanted to hurry and share this good news with his sisters and his brothers—not just about his speech but about the warm welcome he'd experienced. And the delicious food he'd eaten.

Somehow he would get them all to come to church.

No Place for the Blues

Standing in the kitchen, watching them spread old raggedy quilts on the floor for their beds, Ellis Earl was still trying to work up enough nerve to tell his brothers about church and how wonderful the experience had been for him—and might be for them. He had seen during the talent show that followed the speeches that none of the performers even came close to being as good as the Brown Blues. And some of them even performed non-church songs, including popular songs by two Negro rock and roll singers named Chuck Berry and Little Richard. Ellis Earl had reasoned that surely it would be okay for his brothers and Jeannette to sing blues. So he had told Mr. Foster about them.

Mr. Foster said there would be another talent show next month if they wanted to participate. They held them on the third Sunday of every month, for something they called Youth Sunday. Now that Ellis Earl had mentioned the Brown Blues to Mr. Foster, all he needed to do was convince his brothers to show up. But how, when he knew they weren't fond of church and Mama's "church" songs?

Finally, after Ellis Earl had been standing in the doorway of the kitchen to the point of annoyance, Andre, the designated leader of the Brown Blues, turned to him. "You need something outta the kitchen 'foe we go to bed? 'Cause you been standing there for a minute, bro."

Ellis Earl shuffled his feet. "I need to ask y'all something."

"Nah, you can't sleep in here," answered Aaron, the other twin. "Sleep in there with the lil' boys like you always do."

"I wasn't gonna ask that," said Ellis Earl.

"Then what you want?" Raymond, the non-twin, asked gruffly.

"It's about church," said Ellis Earl.

"Go to bed, Earl," said Andre. "You done talked enough 'bout church with Mama and them lil' children already today, filling they heads with dreams. Don't nobody wanna hear no mo' 'bout how much fun you had and how much food you ate."

"My teacher wants y'all to come sing," Ellis Earl blurted out before he lost his nerve.

Andre stopped spreading a quilt on the floor. He stared at Ellis Earl for so long that Ellis Earl thought that he might say yes. But then he shook his head. "Nah, we ain't singing at no church. You know we don't sing no church songs."

"You don't have to sing church songs," said Ellis Earl. "It's a talent show. You can sing whatever you want. Some boys were singing and dancing like Chuck Berry and Little Richard."

"For real?" asked Raymond, his face lighting up.

But Andre waved his hand dismissively at Ellis Earl. "I don't wanna go to no church. I don't wanna go to no talent show at no church. We sing the blues, and soon we gon' be singing it in a club. Lil' mo' practice, and we'll be ready." He folded his quilts as many times as he dared to make his "bed" thicker but still leave enough length to stretch out his lanky body. "You don't see B. B. King up in no church singing, do you?"

Aaron replied, "Beale Street, baby. That's where we goin'. Memphis, Tennessee. Just like B. B., and just like Elvis Presley."

"Man, ain't nobody stud'n Elvis Presley. He don't sing no blues," chided Raymond.

"Yeah, Elvis don't know what he wanna sing," said Andre. "One day he singing rock and roll. The next day he singing church music. Now he playing in movies. We ain't try'na be like that."

"Humph," said Aaron. "I'm try'na be like whoever making money. And Elvis is making money."

"So you'll sing at the church?" piped in Ellis Earl.

"Heck nah," said Andre before Aaron could even shape his mouth to speak. "I lead this group, and I already told you we ain't singing in no church."

"Maybe we could give it a try," said Raymond. "Earl did say some boys was singing like Chuck Berry up in there. The stuff we sing ain't nothing compared to him."

"Yeah, bro," Aaron said, staring at his twin. "No telling who might be up in that church when we sing. Lots of folks got they start in the church."

"Ain't right to use the church that way," said Andre. "It ain't right to take the unholy and mix it with the holy. A church ain't no place for the blues."

"Look, man," his twin pleaded, "we ain't try'na mix no unholy with the holy. We try'na get seen."

Ellis Earl remembered what Mr. Foster had said about his rebuttal, so he tried to use that skill here. "I saw the talent show today. Nobody was as good as the Brown Blues. And the boy that won got a whole bunch of money."

They all gaped at Ellis Earl, shocked.

And so was he—shocked that such a lie had so easily rolled off his tongue. He hadn't meant to do it. It just *happened*. But what could he do now? Especially when they were all staring at him, waiting for more.

"How much?" asked Andre.

Ellis Earl felt sweat roll from his armpits down his sides. Ellis Earl knew he should stop the lie while it was small and tell his brothers he was only kidding, but the excitement in Raymond's eyes made him keep going.

"I don't know how much," he said. "They passed around a bucket and everybody put money in it."

He sneaked his hands behind his back and crossed his fingers. "At the end of the talent show, they gave all the money to the boy. It was a lot of dollar bills."

Raymond's eyes widened even more. He turned to Andre. "We need to do this. Earl just said we better than anybody he heard. We could win some money." He gestured around the kitchen. "Buy some food, man."

"When is this talent show?" Andre asked.

Ellis Earl swallowed some of the tremble from his voice before he spoke. "On the third Sunday in April. Mr. Foster said it was Youth Sunday."

Andre scratched his head methodically as if calculating the days. "Three weeks from now," he said, nodding. "Plenty time to practice." He sighed. "Tell yo' teacher we'll do it. Don't know what we'll wear. Ain't got no fancy clothes like the ones he gave you. But we'll make do."

Smiling, Raymond added, "Who knows? Maybe them church folks'll collect enough money to git us some food *and* some new clothes."

"Long as it's at least enough to buy some food, I'm good," said Andre. "'Cause that's the *only* reason I'm doing this." With that, he pulled back the raggedy blue-and-gray quilt at the top of his pile, lay down, covered himself, and said, "And tell him that the Brown Blues only sing the blues. Sho' hope he don't mind us bringing it to church."

Smiling on the outside but feeling rotten on the inside, Ellis Earl said, "He won't. He'll just be happy to have y'all sing."

His stomach felt as if someone had dropped a couple of bricks in it. He wondered what his brothers would do when they found out the truth. The deacons at Emmanuel African Methodist Episcopal Church had indeed passed around a bucket and collected many dollar bills as an "offering" for the church. But the money had not gone to the winner of the talent show. Like everyone else who had performed at the Easter program, the winner of the talent show had received nothing more than a round of applause.

MONDAY, APRIL 3

See How We Live

THOUGH A WHOLE WEEK had passed since he convinced his brothers to participate in a talent show for which they would win no money, Ellis Earl couldn't shake from his mind the look on Jeannette's face when his brothers had told her about it. Ellis Earl had never seen her so happy. She had been nicer to Ellis Earl and all the younger children in the family ever since.

It was nice to have a new and improved Jeannette, but Ellis Earl felt horrible for the lie he had told. He wanted to fix it. But if he told his brothers and sister the truth, they would hate him more than they ever had before. And what would Mama think when she found out? Ellis Earl shuddered at the thought of how it would break her heart to find out he had played such a terrible trick on his siblings.

The only bright spot in his life was that his nieces and nephews would be going home in another week or so. His oldest brother, Walter Jr., had stopped by on Friday to check on his children and inform them that he would return to pick them up as soon as their other grandmother made it to Mississippi and got settled in. She had decided to leave her factory job at a meat plant in Chicago and come help Sylvia take care of her children until she was able to care for them herself.

At least this time when he stopped by, Junior had brought a sack of food to help feed the family. For that, Ellis Earl was grateful. It wasn't much food, but every little bit helped.

Ellis Earl brought his attention back to the classroom, where Mr. Foster had just spoken.

He wasn't sure what question Mr. Foster had asked, but several of his classmates, including Philip, had raised their hands. Because Philip had raised his hand, Ellis Earl raised his, too.

"Mr. Harper, please tell the class what you know about the name Kennedy," said Mr. Foster.

"I didn't raise my hand," Dale, the boy who was always interrupting others, answered.

"No, you didn't," replied Mr. Foster. "Which is why I called on you."

"Miss Walker?" Mr. Foster called on the next student.

With a stricken look, Deborah Walker replied, "I didn't raise my hand either."

"I'm aware of that fact, Miss Walker," said Mr. Foster.

Mr. Foster continued throughout the class, inquiring of all the students who had not raised their hands. "Every one of you should have raised your hands," he said. "We have discussed Kennedy in this class, and you shouldn't have forgotten the name so easily."

Ellis Earl wished he hadn't raised his hand because then he would've been called upon. He would have been happy to tell his classmates what Mr. Foster had told him: that Miss Mary Ann Wright had asked a senator named Kennedy to come to Mississippi and see that people needed help getting food.

Once Mr. Foster had chastised the students who had not raised their hands, he called upon one who had. Ellis Earl was disappointed that it wasn't him but happy that it wasn't Philip either. It was his new friend, Cora.

"I know about the name John F. Kennedy," Cora answered. "Is that who you're talking about?"

"Wait. Wait. I know 'bout him," Dale interrupted.

With this, several students piped in with "Oh, yeah!" and "Me too!"

Mr. Foster tapped his paddle on his desk three times to get the students' attention. "You all had your chances to speak, so settle down and listen." To Cora he said, "Miss Scott, please tell us what you know about John F. Kennedy."

"I know he's dead," said Cora.

"He was assassinated," Philip interjected.

"No more interruptions, please, Mr. Harris," said Mr. Foster. "You'll have your chance to speak as well."

"Yes, sir," Philip answered, lowering his chin.

"He was assassinated," Cora said, glancing at Philip. "And he was the president."

When Cora was silent for a moment, Mr. Foster prodded, "Anything else?"

Cora answered, "I think he was shot in the head."

"Do you know why he was shot or who shot him?" asked Mr. Foster.

Cora replied, "I know he was shot because he wanted to help colored people, but I don't remember the name of the man who shot him."

Mr. Foster looked at Philip and nodded.

Philip grinned broadly. "John Fitzgerald Kennedy was the thirty-fifth president of the United States. He was assassinated four years ago, in 1963. President Kennedy was assassinated by Lee Harvey Oswald."

"Thank you for today's history lesson, Mr. Harris," said Mr. Foster. He turned to the class. "President Kennedy has a younger brother. Rob—"

Ellis Earl's hand shot up.

Mr. Foster acknowledged him.

Ellis Earl said eagerly, "Robert Kennedy. He's a senator."

Mr. Foster smiled. "Excellent, Mr. Brown. That's correct. Robert Kennedy, the brother of John F. Kennedy, is a United States senator. And next week, he will be coming to Mississippi."

Wows filled the classroom. This included Ellis

Earl. He couldn't believe the senator was actually coming. "Miss Mary Ann Wright did it," he whispered. "She convinced him to come."

"How come he comin' here?" Dale asked.

"Interestingly—"

Ellis Earl raised his hand before Mr. Foster could finish. Mr. Foster called on him.

So overcome with excitement, Ellis Earl could barely stay in his seat. "There is this lady lawyer from Mississippi. Her name is Miss Mary Ann Wright. She went to Washington, DC, and told some senators that we were having a problem buying food in Mississippi. The senators didn't believe her. So she told them to come see for themselves."

"How do *you* know that?" Philip blurted out.

Mr. Foster gave Philip a stern look; then he turned to Ellis Earl. "That's correct, Mr. Brown. Miss *Marian* Wright did indeed convince Senator Robert Kennedy to come to Mississippi. She wants him to hear directly from the people about their struggles to provide for their families."

Dale's eyes bugged. "They ain't comin' to our *houses*, is they?"

Whispers filled the class.

"Calm down," Mr. Foster ordered the class. "I don't think you have to worry about the senator showing up on your front porches. He's coming to Jackson for what's called a Senate subcommittee hearing on poverty." Mr. Foster smiled at Dale, the interrupter. "Since I know what's going through some of your minds, I'll go ahead and tell you what a Senate subcommittee hearing is."

Snickers broke out in the class as they all looked at Dale.

"A Senate subcommittee hearing is when a specific topic, such as poverty in an area like ours, needs to be addressed," said Mr. Foster. "Last month, such a hearing was held in Washington, DC, and some of our people from Mississippi, like Miss Marian Wright, were there to discuss poverty in our state, especially in this area, the Delta. Senator Kennedy finds it hard to believe that anyone's situation could be as dire as they claim, so he's coming here for himself to find out."

Dale snorted. "We po' a'right. I don't know how come he wanna come all the way here to Mississippi to see that."

But their classmate Cassandra said, "I can't believe a real live person from Washington, DC, is coming to Mississippi just to see how we live." She spoke so softly that it took everyone by surprise. They were accustomed to Cassandra speaking boisterously at all times. "I hope he *do* come to my house," she continued. "I *want* him to see how we live. I want him to see that we ain't got but two rooms—one in the front and one in the back. I want him to see that our walls is made of cinder blocks, and Mama say it make her feel like she in a prison.

"I want him to see that bed up in the front room where me and my mama and my grandmama sleep. And I'm gon' show him the spot where my two lil' brothers fix they pallet every night.

"Then I'm gon' take him on to the back room and show him how empty it is. I'm gon' show him that the icebox is empty. I'm gon' show him that the safe is empty. I'm gon' show him that the flour bucket is empty. And the meal and the lard buckets is, too. Then I'm gon' show him that we ain't got a table to eat at for the lil' times that we do have food.

"Yessir," she said, nodding. "I sho' do hope that senator come to my house. I wanna show him exactly how we live."

When she finished, the class applauded, for none of them had ever been bold enough to be that honest about how they lived.

"Thank you for sharing with us, Miss Smith," Mr. Foster said to Cassandra. "Who knows? Perhaps Senator Kennedy *will* take a moment to visit the Delta. Perhaps *yours* will be the lucky home he'll visit."

Ellis Earl was proud of Cassandra for speaking so candidly, yet he himself could never be so vocal about how he lived. Sure, he hoped the senator would make a difference and help people get food, but he, like his classmate Dale, would never want the senator to stop by his house. He felt he would probably die from embarrassment if someone so important saw the shack in which he lived.

After the class calmed down from Cassandra's speech, Cora raised her hand again.

Ellis Earl smiled.

"Yes, Miss Scott," Mr. Foster said eagerly.

"May I share something with the class?" Cora asked.

"Of course," said Mr. Foster.

This time, there were no snickers from the back of the class.

"It's about a senator from a long time ago," said Cora. "His name was Blanche Kelso Bruce."

Mr. Foster's face lit up. "Excellent! Tell us about Blanche Kelso Bruce, Miss Scott."

And just like that, as quickly as Cora's light had started to shine, it dimmed.

She shrank down in her seat and quietly said, "Never mind."

Ellis Earl couldn't believe this was the same Cora who had talked to him so much at church. Even without the teasing, she was too shy to speak up. Ellis Earl decided to encourage her. He raised his hand.

"Yes, Mr. Brown?" said Mr. Foster.

"I know a little bit about Blanche Kelso Bruce," he said. "Maybe we could talk about him together—me and Cora. I mean, Cora and I, sir."

Mr. Foster raised his brows. "Oh?"

"Yes, sir," said Ellis Earl.

"Miss Scott?" said Mr. Foster, still eyeing Ellis Earl suspiciously. "A team effort?"

Furrowing her brows, Cora glanced back at Ellis Earl. He smiled reassuringly.

"Um, okay," she said softly.

As Cora stood before the class, she spoke quickly. "Blanche Kelso Bruce was a slave at first, then he escaped while white folks were busy fighting the Civil War and he moved to Missouri, I think, and built a school for Negro children. After that, he moved to Mississippi, right here in Bolivar County where we live, and became the sheriff. I don't know how that happened since he was a colored man, but it did happen. My daddy said so. After that he became a senator, like what Mr. Robert Kennedy is."

Cora abruptly stopped talking and glanced at Ellis Earl. "You can tell the rest."

Ellis Earl felt a familiar trickle of sweat roll from his armpits and down his sides. There was no "rest." He had no idea who Blanche Kelso Bruce was except for what Cora had just told the class. His ploy was to get her to speak. He wasn't considering the fact that she would expect him to actually speak, too.

"Is there anything you would like to add, Mr. Brown?" said Mr. Foster.

Ellis Earl swallowed. "Um, no, sir. She said everything I was gonna say."

Philip snorted loudly.

"Mr. Harris, is there something *you* would like to share?"

"No, sir," Philip answered.

"Thank you, Miss Scott," Mr. Foster said to Cora. He then addressed the class, "Blanche Kelso Bruce was indeed born a slave in 1841 in Virginia. He escaped during the Civil War, as Miss Scott has said, started a school in Missouri, then continued his own education in Ohio. When the Civil War ended, Mr. Bruce moved to Mississippi, to this very county, and became the sheriff and the tax collector. He was later elected to serve in the United States Senate. He is the only Negro who has ever served a full term as a senator."

Mr. Foster paused and glared at Dale, the interrupting boy. "For those of you who choose to take education for granted, Blanche K. Bruce is a great example of why you should not."

Dale raised his hand. "How did he start a school if he was a runaway slave? I thought slaves couldn't read."

"Some of them could," answered Mr. Foster.

"Like Frederick Douglass," said Philip.

"Wasn't that against the law?" asked another student.

"Of course," replied Mr. Foster. "Which is all the more reason why you should value your *free* education."

Ellis Earl thought about his older siblings—Junior, Aaron, Andre, Raymond, Jeannette. What if they had stayed in school? What if Junior had graduated from high school? Would his life be different? Even though he had a halfway decent job building roads for the county, sometimes he still fell short and could barely provide for his growing family.

Ellis Earl knew then and there that staying in school was what he had to do regardless of whether or not his family needed him to work. Somehow, when he finished sixth grade, he would convince Mama to let him stay in school. If a runaway slave could *start* a school, then surely he, Ellis Earl Brown, should be allowed to finish.

The RFK Welcoming Team

Ellis Earl felt like pinching himself. As he sat with his siblings on the front porch that afternoon, he still had a hard time believing what had happened at recess.

Mr. Foster had asked him, Philip, Dale, Willie, and Jerry—the five of them who had participated in the Easter program—to remain inside. At first Ellis Earl had been disappointed. The weather was nice, and all morning he had been looking forward to the sun hitting his skin because the classroom still held its chill from the night before. But when

Mr. Foster announced that the five of them had been selected to accompany him on a very special trip, the chill melted off Ellis Earl like butter on a hot biscuit. Immediately he knew that this was that "someplace special" that Mr. Foster had referred to when he invited him to the Easter program.

Jackson. To the airport. On Sunday. To see Senator Robert Kennedy.

As Mr. Foster had promised, it was indeed "someplace *very special* with the chance to meet someone *very important*." Ellis Earl had not expected it to be so soon and to meet someone so important. But Mr. Foster had been planning the trip since the moment he heard that the senator might come to Mississippi.

Ellis Earl couldn't wait to tell Mama when she got home. She would be so happy for him. He hadn't uttered a word to his siblings about the trip because he wanted Mama to be the first to know.

He smiled, remembering how on Easter morning Mama had said he was going to be somebody one day. Going to Jackson to the airport to see Senator Robert Kennedy didn't actually make him somebody, but Ellis Earl considered it a step in the right direction. He wondered if Senator Robert

Kennedy was a lawyer like Miss Marian Wright and Mr. Thurgood Marshall. Lawyers seemed to be pretty important people. They helped people, and that's what Ellis Earl wanted to do.

Since the weather was warm, the younger Browns had played outside in the yard that afternoon as they awaited the arrival of the working members of the family. Even Oscar was outside, but he didn't have the strength to play. He sat on an overturned milk crate on the porch. Ellis Earl sat with him. Lucky, the cat, sat between them, purring. He wasn't too shabby for a mangy cat.

Ellis Earl was glad Lucky had followed him and Carrie Ann home. And he was even gladder they hadn't forced him away.

Lucky was the reason Oscar wanted to be outside.

Mama said the fresh air and sunshine would help Oscar regain his strength. Ellis Earl sure hoped so. His brother looked like he was fading away.

Ellis Earl was supposed to be reading *Charlie and the Chocolate Factory*. All the excitement over the past week—the Easter program and the talent show deception—had caused him to fall behind in his reading. Today, instead of reading, he couldn't help staring at Oscar. Oscar had never been a big fellow, but now it seemed to Ellis Earl that his arms and legs were mere skin and bones. His legs appeared so frail that Ellis Earl doubted he could run from the porch to the road.

With Oscar simply sitting there, rubbing Lucky's back and staring blankly at the other children playing in the yard, Ellis Earl offered to entertain him by reading from his book. Since Oscar had become ill back in January, Ellis Earl had been trying to convince him to keep up with his schoolwork by reading pages from his textbooks. But Oscar had lacked both the strength and the will to do any kind of reading during his months of illness. Knowing how much *Charlie and the Chocolate Factory* had stirred his own love of reading, Ellis Earl thought perhaps it could help Oscar, too.

He offered to read it to him.

"What's it about?" Oscar asked.

"A boy named Charlie Bucket," said Ellis Earl. "His family lives in a small house like ours. They only have two rooms. And all four of his grandparents live in the house with him and his mama and daddy. And all the grandparents sleep in one bed. Charlie and his mama and daddy even sleep on mattresses on the floor like we do."

"What kind of story is *that*?" asked Oscar, sitting up a little straighter. "How can four grown people sleep in one bed? What if one of 'em fart?"

"Like you do every night!" Ellis Earl said. Both boys laughed.

"What else?" asked Oscar after they stopped laughing.

"Well, there's this man named Willy Wonka. He owns the chocolate factory. Charlie is too poor to buy chocolate, so he just stands outside the gate and watches the knee-high people inside making the chocolate."

"Sound like a real good story," said Oscar. "Yeah, read it to me!"

Ellis Earl smiled. "You'll like Charlie Bucket. He's just a regular boy like us." He opened the book and started at the beginning. "'Chapter One: Here Comes Charlie . . .'"

By the time the working members of the family arrived home, Ellis Earl had read to the fourth chapter. It was the fastest he had ever read. And Oscar had enjoyed hearing Charlie Bucket's story as much as Ellis Earl had enjoyed reading it.

Mama's face looked weary, and Ellis Earl couldn't wait to brighten it with his news. He waited until she was fully in the house, in the middle room where she always went first. He approached her as she sat on the side of the bed and removed her worn black shoes.

"How you feelin', Mama?"

Mama rubbed the bottom of her calloused foot and smiled up at Ellis Earl. "Tired," she said, shaking her head.

"What kinda work you do today?"

"Some washin' for Miss Josie Spears. And a lil' bit of cleanin' for Miss Abigail Hines."

Ellis Earl placed his hand on her shoulder. "Sorry about the job with Mrs. Chalmers."

"No need to be sorry. Ain't yo' fault. The good Lord sent the rain. And He always know what He doing. Besides, Miss Lucinda back at work anyway. That old woman strong as a ox. Can't nothin' keep her down. Not even the flu."

"I'm glad you were able to find some work today," said Ellis Earl.

Mama smiled. "I got a good reputation. And I do good work. Most of the time when I go knockin' on a do', the missus will let me help out her maid at half the pay."

"Today was your lucky day, Mama," Ellis Earl said. "You had two jobs."

"I 'on know 'bout lucky," Mama said. "That washin' job didn't pay 'nuff to buy a can of peaches with."

Both Mama and Ellis Earl laughed. This was a joke the family made when one of them worked nearly half a day and barely got paid.

"I got something to tell you," Ellis Earl said.

Mama's forehead creased. "What is it, baby? Nothing bad, I hope."

"It's something good," said Ellis Earl, beaming.

Mama's face relaxed.

"You know how my teacher, Mr. Foster, likes to take us places we never been before, like to church and whatnot?"

"Mm-hmm," Mama answered as she went back to rubbing her tired feet.

"Well, this time he's taking us to Jackson!" said Ellis Earl.

Mama stopped rubbing her feet. "Jackson? What for?"

Ellis Earl was disappointed that Mama wasn't as excited as he expected her to be. But he forged on. "Something real special," he said. "A real important man is coming from Washington, DC, on Sunday, and some people from Mr. Foster's church are going to the airport in Jackson to see him when he gets off the airplane. Mr. Foster's gonna take some of us with him, and we're gonna be a part of his welcoming team. He called it the RFK Welcoming Team!"

"Who this man? The president of the United States or something?"

"No, ma'am," Ellis Earl said, shaking his head. "But his brother was the president. And he's a senator. But his brother died. Somebody shot him 'cause he wanted to help colored people."

"You talkin' 'bout Kennedy?"

"Yes, ma'am. John F. Kennedy. Uncle Joseph got his picture on his wall."

"His brother Bobby Kennedy?" asked Mama. "That who coming to Mississippi?"

"Is Bobby Kennedy the same as Robert Kennedy?" asked Ellis Earl.

Mama nodded. "He is."

"Then yes, ma'am. That's him," Ellis Earl said, smiling big.

Mama's face brightened a bit. "Well now, ain't that something. Mr. Bobby Kennedy coming to Mississippi."

Ellis Earl's heart raced. "Can I go?"

And just like that, Mama's expression dimmed. "I don't know, Earl. What if something happen to you? That's a long drive to Jackson."

"How far is it?" asked Ellis Earl.

Mama shrugged. "I don't know exactly. I just know it's a long way from here. Too far for me to be lettin' you ride off with somebody I don't really know."

"Mama!" Ellis Earl exclaimed. "You let me and Carrie Ann ride to school with Mr. Foster every day!"

Mama frowned. "That's just to town and back."

"You let me go to church with him."

"That's in town, too."

Ellis Earl poked out his lip. "I bet the other boys' mamas are gonna let them go. I'll be the only one who won't get to go."

"What you gon' wear? You ain't got no decent

clothes to be going to see no senator at the airport."

"I got the pants and shirt from Easter," said Ellis Earl.

"I need some time to think about this, Earl."

Mama's words nearly broke Ellis Earl's heart. "*Why?*" he asked, tears brimming his eyes.

"Do you know why President Kennedy was shot?"

Biting his lip to fight back the tears, Ellis Earl nodded.

"Don't you know some of these white folks in Mississippi hate his brother just as much as they hated him?"

With the back of his hands, Ellis Earl swiped away the tears that had begun rolling down his face.

"Yo' teacher 'n 'em ain't gon' be the only ones at that airport in Jackson," Mama continued. "White folks gon' be there, too. And some of them gon' be some mean and hateful white folks."

"But what if they ain't?" asked Ellis Earl, his bottom lip trembling. "What if only the nice white folks like Miss Abigail is there?"

"Don't mistake need for niceness. Ol' Miss

Abigail ain't nice just 'cause she lets colored women clean her house. Miss Abigail let colored women clean her house 'cause she too lazy to clean it herself.

"There might be some nice white folks at the airport on Sunday. But I bet you a dollar, that ain't neither one of us got, that the mean ones gon' be there, too. And that's a dangerous place for a little colored boy like yo'self to be."

The tears that began slowly quickened down Ellis Earl's face.

"I know you sad, honey," said Mama. "But you don't know how dangerous it is when white folks try to help colored folks. That white woman I was working for when Kennedy got shot—know what she said when she heard the news?"

When Ellis Earl didn't answer, Mama said, "She said, 'Thank the good Lord, somebody stopped him.' Then she *laughed*, Earl."

This caused Ellis Earl to shudder. But he still wanted to go to Jackson.

"Too many of these white people down here don't like them Kennedys," Mama said. "I ain't letting you go to Jackson to no airport where one of 'em gonna be. It's too dangerous."

Ellis Earl tried to block out Mama's words as he imagined Philip and Dale and Jerry and Willie riding with Mr. Foster all the way down to Jackson. He imagined Mr. Foster packing a lunch for them to eat along the way. Or he might even stop at a diner and let them sit inside and eat. He would let them buy hamburgers and French fries and get fountain drinks like Coca-Cola or root beer. He would teach them important things along the way. He would talk about the importance of getting an education. Then they would get to Jackson and go to the airport and watch an important man get off an airplane and set foot on Mississippi dirt.

Ellis Earl didn't care if dangerous white people would be there. He didn't even care if the Ku Klux Klan was there. He still wanted to be there. He wanted to be there because all the other boys would be there. He wanted to be there because Mr. Foster had said Cora *and* her brothers, plus a few other girls from school, would be there. He wanted to be there because it would make him feel like somebody special—like he was a part of something big. He wanted to be there for his siblings, who never got to go anywhere special. He wanted to be there for Oscar, who couldn't go anywhere at all.

He tried reasoning with Mama. "You have to let me go. You said I was gon' be somebody, but you scared to let me go to Jackson. How can I be somebody if you won't even let me go see an important man at the airport? How can any of us be somebody if we don't ever leave this house except to go to school or do like you do and hope somebody give you some work?"

The second the words left his mouth, Ellis Earl knew that, even though they were right, they were also wrong. He knew that, with them, he had crushed Mama's feelings.

He knew that he should apologize. But he couldn't. Not when his own dreams lay crushed beneath the weight of his mama's fears.

Enough Fighting Going On in the World

Oscar had so enjoyed the reading of *Charlie and the Chocolate Factory* that he begged Ellis Earl to read to him again.

Ellis Earl was not really in a mood to read. Mama had just killed his dream of going someplace special and seeing someone special, and he had insulted her by implying that what she did every day was not important to the family's survival. Yet he read anyway, because all the little children had gathered around the mattress to hear about the life of an imaginary boy named Charlie Bucket.

"I wonder how Charlie gon' get that ticket if he only get one candy bar a year," said Oscar. He was lying on his side on the mattress, propped up on one elbow. It was the brightest Ellis Earl had seen him look in a while.

"I bet he gon' get it in his birthday bar," said Carrie Ann, her eyes beaming with anticipation.

"Nuh-uh," said seven-year-old Beatrice. "I bet he ain't gon' get one at all. He ain't goin' to the chocolate factory."

Carrie Ann clucked her tongue. "The book wouldn't be called *Charlie and the Chocolate Factory* if Charlie wasn't gon' get to go to the factory."

Ellis Earl yelled, "Will y'all just let me read, please?"

As the nine children surrounding him quieted down, Ellis Earl read, without much emotion, about how excited the four old grandparents were on the morning of Charlie's birthday.

"You ain't reading the same as you did at first," said Oscar. "You should be sounding excited. Charlie 'bout to open that candy bar, and he 'on know if it gon' have a golden ticket in it or not. I'm gon' be excited if I get anything at all on my birthday on Sunday. So I know Charlie excited."

"Yeah, Earl," said Carrie Ann. "Even I can do better than you is, and I'm just in the third grade."

Ellis Earl stood suddenly and slammed the book shut.

Carrie Ann sprang up from the mattress. "What is you doin'?"

"I'm done reading to y'all," said Ellis Earl. "If y'all don't like my reading, then get your own books from your own teachers and read 'em your own selves."

"That ain't fair!" cried Oscar. "I don't even go to school no mo', so how I'm s'posed to get some books from my teacher?"

"And how you jes' gon' stop like that?" said Carrie Ann. "We wanna know if Charlie gon' find that golden ticket."

"Well, I guess you won't ever know," said Ellis Earl.

"Gimme that book," said Carrie Ann. "I'll finish readin' it myself." She grabbed at the book, but Ellis Earl quickly moved it out of her reach.

He hugged it to his chest. "It's my book, and I'll read it when I want to."

Oscar collapsed down on the mattress. "Don't be selfish, Earl," he said, breathlessly. "We wanna know what happen next."

Ellis Earl knew he was being selfish because

he was being selfish on purpose. Mr. Foster had gotten his hopes up, and Mama had dashed them. He knew it was wrong, but he decided to inflict the same pain upon his siblings and nieces and nephews.

But as he began to walk away, Carrie Ann tackled him and knocked him to the floor.

Ellis Earl landed on his stomach, and his book flew from his hand.

Carrie Ann snatched the book before he could grab it. "I got it!" she yelled, waving the book in the air.

"Read it! Read it!" cried the little ones.

Ellis Earl stumbled to his feet and grabbed at his book—right as Carrie Ann opened it.

RIIIIP!

"Ooooh!" cried all the little children.

With three pages of his beloved book in his hand, Ellis Earl dropped to the floor and fell into a fit of tears. "Look what you made me do!" he yelled at Carrie Ann as he held up the pages to her.

Carrie Ann stood staring at the book with its three missing pages. The other children gaped at Ellis Earl as he bawled.

That night, as he stuffed the ripped pages back

inside, he felt that his precious book would never be the same. It was almost as if a part of him had been ripped out—like his heart maybe. The youngest of the little children had fallen asleep, and Oscar, too, had dozed off. Only Ellis Earl, Carrie Ann, Beatrice, and Deidra sat on the floor of the front room in the glow of the kerosene lamp and listened to the sound of the Brown Blues harmonizing from the middle room. They were preparing for the talent show in a couple of weeks. Ellis Earl still felt bad about deceiving them, but he surely wasn't going to tell them the truth now and add to his own troubles.

"My children sho' can sing," Mama said softly.

"You sing real good, too, Mama," said Beatrice. "When we go back to church, you can sing in the choir like Earl said."

All the younger children had been talking about going to church now that the Brown Blues had agreed to perform in the talent show. When Mama smiled at Beatrice, Ellis Earl could tell that she was giving that idea some serious thought. Yet he remembered what she'd said about not having proper clothes, which reminded him of what Raymond had said about the nonexistent prize money: “Maybe them church folks’ll collect enough money to git us some food *and* some new clothes.”

Guilt hit him so hard this time that it made him shiver. How disappointed everyone would be when they found out he had lied.

Maybe I should just tell them now and get this over with.

But he didn’t. He *couldn’t*. They would all hate him. And he didn’t think he could take that now, when he was already sad about not going to Jackson.

“I bet one day Jeannette ’n ’em gon’ be famous and be on the radio,” said Deidra.

“They already sound like they is,” said Beatrice.

“They *are*,” corrected Ellis Earl.

“Nah, they ain’t,” said Deidra. “They in the middle room. They ain’t on no radio.”

Carrie Ann rolled her eyes at Ellis Earl and said to Deidra, “That ain’t what he meant. He trying to tell people how to talk. You ain’t all that proper, Ellis Earl. Sometimes you don’t talk right neither.”

“I talk better than you,” said Ellis Earl.

Carrie Ann positioned her mouth to respond, but Mama stopped her. “Y’all cut all that nonsense out," she said. "Enough fighting going on in the world already without y'all adding to it."

Ellis Earl considered Mama's words. "Sorry," he muttered to his sisters. "And sorry I didn't finish reading the book to y'all today. I was being selfish." He made a promise to himself to try to do better.

"You sho' was," Carrie Ann said, crossing her arms over her chest. "That's how come the pages got tore out, 'cause you was being so selfish."

"Carrie Ann Brown," said Mama. "Lil' girl, if you don't stop being so doggone contrary, I'm gon' tan yo' hide. Now apologize to Ellis Earl."

Carrie Ann pouted. "Well, it is his fault. We was all having a good time listenin' to the story, and he had to go and spoil it by being selfish. If anybody should get a whuppin', it should be him."

"Bee, go get my strap," Mama said to Beatrice.

The children gasped. Mama rarely used her strap.

"Nooo!" cried Carrie Ann. "I apologize. I *apologize*!" She fell on the floor before Ellis Earl. "I'm sorry I made you tear yo' book! I'm sorry I was being mean! I won't be mean no mo' tonight. I promise!"

"What about tomorrow?" asked Mama.

"And the next day?" asked Ellis Earl.

Carrie Ann plopped back down on her bottom, crossed her arms over her chest again, and declared, "I don't know what kind of person I'm gon' be tomorrow. So I can't make no promises."

Mama shook her head. She said to Beatrice, who was still standing and wondering whether she should go get the strap, "Sit down, Bee. Only God can help this child."

Ellis Earl smiled at Mama. "You're a good mama," he said. "I'm sorry about what I said today."

"It's okay," Mama said, smiling back. "I know you didn't mean it. It was the hurt in your heart that made you do it."

Ellis Earl smiled at Mama, but he also knew there was another thing he had to make right with his sister. "Carrie Ann?" he said.

"What?" Carrie Ann answered, eyeing him sideways.

"You can be a lawyer if you want, 'cause girls can be lawyers, too."

"Humph," said Carrie Ann. "I already knew that. You the one who didn't."

TUESDAY, APRIL 4

Just Walk Slow

NOT WANTING TO BE PULLED into conversation with any of the other children in Mr. Foster's car during the ride home, Ellis Earl slumped down in his seat. Carrie Ann was talking enough for both of them anyway, telling all their business, such as the fact that they had cornbread with molasses for supper the night before.

"Who eat cornbread and molasses?" Larry asked.

"Nobody!" said a girl named Sharon. "You eat molasses with biscuits, not cornbread. That's nasty!"

"Well, Jeannette didn't have enough flour to make no biscuits," retorted Carrie Ann. "So we had cornbread, and we can eat cornbread and molasses if we want."

Carrie Ann next told Mr. Foster that Ellis Earl had ripped pages from his book. She said it in a way that made it sound as if he did it on purpose, as if he didn't appreciate the gift he had been given.

Ellis Earl was happy when their road came into view. He couldn't wait to get out of Mr. Foster's car. Who knew what Carrie Ann might say next?

Besides escaping his little sister telling all their business, Ellis Earl couldn't wait to get home so he could show his older sister the gift he had brought her. A book from Mr. Foster's library. A book that Mr. Foster said Jeannette could keep for herself.

Still thinking about what Mama had said about all the fighting going on in the world, Ellis Earl also got to thinking about the look on Jeannette's face when he caught her reading *Charlie and the Chocolate Factory*. He still felt bad for almost saying she couldn't read. What she had said was true: just because you never see someone reading doesn't mean they can't. In Jeannette's case, she didn't have anything to read. In his case, he had not discovered what he wanted to read. Until he met Charlie.

For Jeannette, he had chosen a Nancy Drew mystery. Since his friend Philip had suggested the Hardy Boys mystery *The Secret of the Old Mill* to him, he had selected *The Secret of the Old Clock* for Jeannette. He hoped she would like it. And she'd even have time to read it once Junior's little ones returned home.

As they approached the road leading to their house, rather than slowing down, Mr. Foster kept going at the same speed. When he reached the winding dirt road that led to their house, he drove right past it.

"Mr. Foster?" Ellis Earl inquired.

But before he could say more, Carrie Ann yelled, "Hey! You missed our house!"

"I know," said Mr. Foster. "I'm dropping you off last today."

"How come?" asked Carrie Ann.

"I need to speak with your mother," said Mr. Foster, glancing at Carrie Ann in the rearview mirror.

Carrie Ann's eyes bugged. "Is Ellis Earl in trouble?"

Ellis Earl flinched. "Am I?" he asked.

"No, Mr. Brown, you're not in trouble," said Mr. Foster. "Neither is your sister," he added when he noticed how Ellis Earl glared at Carrie Ann. "I need to speak with your mother about Sunday."

Ellis Earl's heart skipped. He didn't know how Mama would feel about Mr. Foster coming to the house to ask about him going to Jackson. After he had told Mr. Foster that he couldn't go, Mr. Foster had said that Mama didn't understand the significance of the trip and that he would speak to her about it. Ellis Earl had no idea he would come to the house. Of course, how else was he supposed to speak to her about it? They had no telephone on which he could call her.

Knowing it would be a long ride home, Ellis Earl settled down even deeper into his seat and watched his sister's mouth run like a rushing river. She even conjured up a few tales that were so bizarre that Ellis Earl wondered whether the other children in the carpool actually believed her!

By the time Mr. Foster's station wagon pulled into the yard of the Brown home, it was almost time for the working members of the family to arrive. Jeannette, of course, was already there. She stood on the porch, her fists planted firmly at her hips, a frown draping her face like heavy curtains.

"Jeannette sho' is mad," said Carrie Ann as they emerged from the car.

Ellis Earl said nothing. He wasn't sure whether he should invite Mr. Foster in or have him wait in the car. The latter was the ruder of the two options, but the former was the more humiliating.

Ellis Earl pictured the scene: The darkened front room with a wood stove in the corner and a sunken mattress beside it. The covering on the mattress is disheveled because underneath is a sick boy—or perhaps this is one of his better days and Oscar is actually sitting on one of the two rickety, hand-me-down chairs in the front room. Then there are the buckets, overturned to mimic tables. They are at least covered with cloth so that only those who made the makeshift tables know that they are actually buckets. Atop one table sits a kerosene lamp, which is probably lit since it's evening time and the room has grown darker. And the floor, wooden and splintered, is uneven in places but hopefully swept clean because the housekeeper, Jeannette, is one for cleanliness. Will the little children, though, be clean? Yes, Jeannette is one for cleanliness, but not when it comes to the little children. With there being so many of them, dirty noses and faces (and perhaps a dirty diaper on the littlest one) are a real possibility.

And what if Jeannette asked about the prize money for the talent show? He certainly had to stop that before it happened.

Ellis Earl turned to Mr. Foster. "Wait here. I need to talk to my sister."

Mr. Foster, with a caring smile, nodded.

Carrie Ann bolted toward the porch. "Earl's teacher came home with us!"

"I can see that," Jeannette said. "This about that talent show?" she asked Ellis Earl when he reached the porch.

"No," he said quickly. "He wants to talk to Mama. It probably ain't a good time to talk about the talent show either. So don't ask him nothing."

"You in trouble?"

"Nope."

Jeannette didn't believe him. "What you do?" she asked.

"I didn't do nothing," said Ellis Earl.

"Then why yo' teacher here?"

"I just told you he needs to talk to Mama," said Ellis Earl.

"He ain't in trouble," interjected Carrie Ann. "Mr. Foster said so."

"He bet' not be," said Jeannette. She said to Carrie Ann, "Go in there and take that stanky diaper off Prince."

She said again to Ellis Earl, "You bet' not be in trouble."

"I *ain't*."

Jeannette raised her brows. "You just gon' leave him in the car?"

"I told him I needed to talk to you first."

"Well, you just did, so go tell him to come in."

Ellis Earl hesitated. "Can't we wait till Carrie Ann finish changing Prince?"

"Boy, go git yo' teacher," snapped Jeannette. "Just walk slow."

Ellis Earl remembered the book. The Nancy Drew mystery. Maybe this gift would put Jeannette in a better mood.

Instead, when he handed her the book, Jeannette scowled at him. "What's this?"

Ellis Earl smiled encouragingly. "A book for

you. I got it from Mr. Foster. He said you can have it."

As Jeannette studied the cover of the book, her face softened. Ellis Earl thought he saw a smile. He expected a huge thank-you to follow. Instead Jeannette yelled at him, "Didn't I tell you to go git yo' teacher?"

It seemed their tardiness had brought the old, mean Jeannette back, and not even a gift could change that. Not wanting to antagonize her more, Ellis Earl scurried off the porch to invite Mr. Foster into the house.

Sitting on the old rocking chair, Mr. Foster, in his creased gray slacks and polished black shoes, looked as uncomfortable as Ellis Earl felt. Ellis Earl had remembered being at Uncle Joseph's house and his wife offering them something to drink. He wanted to do that, but all they had was water, and he couldn't trust that one of the little children hadn't been drinking water straight from the dipper rather than dipping water from the bucket and into a glass as Mama had instructed them all to do.

So Ellis Earl, along with the others, sat there, waiting for the sound of footsteps on the front porch. The whole house seemed to let out a breath when voices were heard in the yard. Ellis Earl rushed outside to greet them. Mama would be worried when she saw Mr. Foster's car parked in the yard. Plus, he wanted to make sure his brothers knew he wasn't there to talk about the talent show.

The look on Mama's face confirmed Ellis Earl's thoughts. "My teacher wants to talk to you about Sunday," he said.

Mama paused at the steps. "Earl, I done told you that you can't go. Now why you go and get yo' teacher to come all the way to the house to try to sway me otherwise?"

"I didn't," Ellis Earl said, shaking his head. "He just said he was coming to talk to you."

Mr. Foster stood when Mama entered the house. He greeted her with a handshake.

A look of embarrassment shrouded Mama's face. "Good evening, Mr. Foster," she said. "What brangs you all the way out here on a Tuesday evening?" She didn't invite him to sit.

While the little children remained in the front room, the rest of the family shuffled on to the back of the house. Well, to the middle room, actually, where they would be able to eavesdrop.

Standing near the front door, Mr. Foster said

to Mama, "Mrs. Brown, Ellis told me that you have denied him the privilege of traveling to Jackson with me and a group of his peers."

Mama responded, "I ain't denying him no privileges. I just said he couldn't go. You make it sound like I'm trying to punish him or something."

Mr. Foster, no doubt realizing his tone had been a bit accusing, reframed his argument. "Going to Jackson to the airport would be a great opportunity for Ellis to have an experience outside of his community. I chose only five students to go on this important field trip, so I consider it a privilege for him to go. I would hate for him to not have this experience."

Ellis Earl could tell from the look in Mama's eyes that she was exhausted and ready to head to the middle room, plop down on the side of the bed, remove her shoes, massage her aching feet for a bit, then lie flat on her back for a few moments to catch her breath before dealing with her menagerie of children. Instead here was his teacher throwing big words at her, trying to convince her to allow him to go to an airport to see a white man get off a plane.

"Mr. Foster?" Ellis Earl interrupted. "I thank

you for asking me to go with you. I feel honored to be chosen." He paused and glanced at his tired mama. "But if my mama don't want me to go, then I don't want to go. I will honor her wishes."

Lines crisscrossed Mr. Foster's forehead. Ellis Earl couldn't tell whether he was confused or angry. If he was angry, then Ellis Earl wouldn't blame him. He had sat in that dark room waiting for Mama to show up and state a case for Ellis Earl to attend the trip, and Ellis Earl had just told him he didn't want to. Ungrateful is what he was.

"He can go," Mama said tiredly.

"Ma'am?" said both Mr. Foster and Ellis Earl together.

Mama motioned to one of the chairs. "Please sit down, Mr. Foster."

Mama sat, too. Ellis Earl sat cross-legged on the floor near her feet.

Mama sat silently for a moment, staring at her hands. Ellis Earl wanted to say something, but he didn't know what to say.

When Mama finally spoke, she had tears in her eyes. "Mr. Foster, first of all, thank you for all you do for my boy and for Carrie Ann, too. Pickin' 'em up every day, takin' 'em to school and everything.

I 'on know how they would get there otherwise with no bus comin' this far out. I had thought 'bout takin' Earl outta school in a couple of years when he turn thirteen. Times is hard. Work hard to find. We need everybody's hand to help out to keep food on the table."

When she saw the distraught look on Ellis Earl's face, Mama paused, reached down to him, and patted his shoulder. Ellis Earl lowered his head. A tear escaped his eye.

"Son, I ain't gon' take you outta school," Mama said.

She turned to Mr. Foster. "I see how Earl be brangin' books home from the library he say you keep in yo' classroom. He brang the books to the little children and read to 'em. My grandbaby Vera only three, and she can read all them books 'bout that little curious monkey. Earl taught her that. And I been hearing him read that Charlie book to all the children. It do my heart good, especially when Oscar asked him to read to him.

"What I'm trying to say, Mr. Foster, is that I want Earl to make it," said Mama. "And I can see you tryin' to help. So I'm gon' let him go to Jackson. And I'm gon' let him see Mr. Kennedy when he get off that plane. And I'm gon' let him be a part of yo' welcoming team."

Mr. Foster smiled broadly. Ellis Earl had never seen him smile so big. "Thank you, Mrs. Brown," he said.

"But you got to promise me one thing," Mama said. "Promise me you ain't gon' let nobody hurt my son."

"Mrs. Brown, I promise to not let anything happen to Ellis or any other child in my care. I will protect them like I would protect my own life."

Mr. Foster was smiling. But Mama wasn't. The look on her face told Ellis Earl that no amount of assurance from Mr. Foster could erase the fear from her heart.

SUNDAY, APRIL 9

It's a Miracle!

Ellis Earl had not slept the whole night—not because he was nervous like Mama, but because he was too terribly excited. What boy could sleep when something so important awaited him the next morning?

He felt like Charlie, who, at the point where Ellis Earl had stopped reading to the little children, was on his way to Mr. Willy Wonka's chocolate factory. It was the fastest Ellis Earl had ever read. He discovered that the more he read—and the more delicious the story became—the faster he read.

As the Brown siblings had predicted, Charlie

had indeed found a golden ticket, but not in the way they expected. And he found it just when the Browns thought he wouldn't. And he found it just when the Buckets needed it most. Charlie and his family were starving! Mr. Bucket had lost his job and was only able to earn a few pennies by shoveling snow in the streets. They were down to one slice of bread per person for breakfast, a half of a boiled potato each for lunch (sometimes), and maybe nothing for dinner.

Ellis Earl knew exactly how Charlie felt.

"It's a miracle!" Oscar had shouted when Ellis Earl read about Charlie finding the ticket.

And together, they had all shouted "Yay!" and pumped their fists in the air to celebrate Charlie.

They were just as excited as the four old grandparents in the book. Even Jeannette came rushing from the middle room, with one-year-old Prince on her hip, yelling, "What happened? What's going on?" Of course, when the children told her, she waved them off and said it was just a silly book and scolded them for acting as if Charlie Bucket were a real boy worthy of so much commotion.

Yet Ellis Earl had seen how much Jeannette was enjoying the Nancy Drew mystery *The Secret of the Old Clock.* She had her nose buried between the pages of that book every chance she got. Ellis Earl decided to ask Mr. Foster for another book, as he was sure Jeannette would be finished reading the one she had in a few more days. She seemed to enjoy that book as much as she enjoyed rehearsing for the talent show next week. The nice Jeannette was back. Ellis Earl hoped she'd still be nice after she found out there was no money for the winner of the talent show.

With a smile, Ellis Earl shrugged off Jeannette's thoughts about Charlie not being a real boy. To him, Charlie was as real as any boy he knew. And to him and to the little children, he was worth cheering on.

As was Ellis Earl.

He was a hero to the little children. Jackson, Mississippi, might as well have been Chicago, Illinois, or Washington, DC, or Mr. Wonka's chocolate factory as far as they were concerned. None of them had a chance of going to any of those places. But Ellis Earl was going. And he was going to see a very important person. Like Charlie, he felt as if he had been handed a golden ticket.

And like Charlie, whom the grandparents had

kept up past midnight, Ellis Earl couldn't sleep. He knew it wasn't nearly time to get up, as he had not heard even one bird chirp outside. Nor had he heard Lucky scratching and meowing at the front door, something he was prone to do before the sun arose in the eastern sky. So Ellis Earl rolled over on his side and tried to sleep.

He wanted desperately to sleep now because he didn't want to fall asleep on the way to Jackson. He wanted to see everything between his little town of Wilsonville and the big city of Jackson. Plus, Oscar was counting on him to bring back every detail of the trip. He said it would be the best birthday present ever, which made Ellis Earl feel better, as he had promised Oscar a present. And he couldn't deliver. Not even a simple candy bar, like the Buckets gave Charlie every year.

Mr. Foster had said that the trip would take more than three hours, and that they would travel through places called Belzoni and Yazoo City. Ellis Earl remembered Mr. Foster telling them about a colored man getting killed in Belzoni for helping other colored people register to vote. But that had been a long time ago, back in 1955, the year Ellis Earl was born.

Mr. Foster said that many colored people were still afraid to register to vote. Ellis Earl figured Mama was one of those people since he had never heard her even talk about voting. But Ellis Earl didn't mind Mama keeping herself safe. They had already lost their father; they didn't need to lose their mother, too. He just hoped the RFK Welcoming Team wouldn't encounter any trouble when they reached the city of Belzoni.

After a while, and without him knowing when, sleep embraced Ellis Earl like a long-lost relative who had finally come home. An hour later, when Mama gently shook his shoulder, he startled.

"Earl, wake up, baby. You gon' be late and not be ready when Mr. Foster get here."

Ellis Earl sprang straight up on the mattress. How could he have fallen asleep so deeply? How could he have missed the birds chirping and Lucky scratching?

He scrambled to his feet. "What time is it?"

"Calm down," said Mama. "It's still early. I just didn't want you to oversleep. I wanted you to take yo' time getting properly cleaned up. I already got you some water heated up for washing. You can go on in the kitchen and wash up."

When Ellis Earl hesitated, Mama said, "Go on. Yo' brothers won't mind you in there with the lamp on this one morning. They understand how important this is."

She smiled, placed her hand on Ellis Earl's cheek, and said, "This trip mean a lot to all of us, Earl."

"It does?" asked Ellis Earl.

Mama nodded. "It sho' do."

"You ain't scared about it?"

"A lil' bit. But I prayed 'bout it and asked the good Lord to protect you. I hope he'll honor my request."

"He will, Mama. He'll keep me safe."

When Ellis Earl returned to the front room, neatly dressed in the clothes that Mr. Foster had given him for Easter, Mama invited him to come sit in the chair beside her. The smile on her face told Ellis Earl how proud she was of him.

"I have something for you," she said, reaching over to the makeshift table for something tied in her prized lace handkerchief, the one that she kept folded in her pocketbook at all times.

Ellis Earl leaned toward her. "Something for me? What is it?"

"Here," Mama said, handing him the handkerchief.

Ellis Earl beamed when he untied the handkerchief. "Doughnuts!" he said in a whisper shout in order to not wake the little ones. "For me?" he asked, smiling at Mama. "Both of 'em?"

"'Course they for you," Mama answered gently.

Ellis Earl took a bite of one of the doughnuts. Though it was a bit stale, Ellis Earl closed his eyes and savored every chew.

"Where did you get them from?" he asked, and nibbled slowly, so as not to eat them up too quickly.

"Miss Abigail," answered Mama.

"She gave you doughnuts?"

Mama smiled mischievously. "Well, she didn't actually give 'em to me."

Ellis Earl stopped chewing. "You stole 'em, Mama?"

"I wouldn't exactly call it stealing neither. More like I just took 'em out of the bread box and put 'em in my handkerchief when she wasn't looking."

"I think that's the same as stealing," said Ellis Earl.

"How 'bout we say I stole 'em from her dog then?"

"Huh?"

"That's what she was gon' do with 'em anyway," said Mama. "What she didn't eat, her dog would. So I didn't steal from Miss Abigail. I stole 'em from her big ugly dog, Brutus."

At that, Ellis Earl couldn't help but laugh.

"You're like Charlie's mama," he said.

"Who Charlie?"

"You know, from the book I've been reading to Oscar and the little children."

"You know them ain't real peoples, don't you?"

"I know. But they *feel* real to me."

Mama smiled. "How is I like Charlie's mama then?"

"You made a sacrifice for me. When Charlie's family was starving and they could only have one piece of bread each for breakfast, Charlie's mama tried to give Charlie her piece of bread. But Charlie didn't take it because he wanted his mama to eat, too." Ellis Earl handed Mama the handkerchief. "That's why I saved you one of the doughnuts."

"You eat both of 'em. Fill up. I don't want you going on the road with yo' teacher hungry."

"Mr. Foster will bring food. He always brings food."

“That’s fine and well,” said Mama. “But my boy gon’ already be full when he get here.”

Ellis Earl patted his stomach. “I’m already full.”

Mama smiled. “I’m gon’ be like Charlie then. I ain’t gon’ take yo’ serving of bread.”

Ellis Earl glanced over at the disheveled lump of quilts on the mattress. “Then save it for Oscar. I promised him something for his birthday. I guess this doughnut can be his present.”

The Word Is *Corridor*

"Good morning, Mr. Foster," Ellis Earl said as he eased into the front seat of the station wagon.

With the morning sun highlighting his happy face, Mr. Foster nodded and said, "Top of the morning to you, Mr. Brown."

Ellis Earl was surprised, and happy, to see that none of the other boys had been picked up yet—especially Philip. He relaxed into the seat and let the joy that was bubbling up inside his heart rise to his face and form a smile on his lips.

Since the drive was going to be such a long one, Ellis Earl had brought his book with him.

Mr. Foster seemed pleased to see it sitting in Ellis Earl's lap.

"How's the reading coming along?"

"Very good," said Ellis Earl. "I'm at the part where Charlie is about to go to the factory."

"Is that so?"

Beaming, Ellis Earl said, "Yes, sir. And it's a sunny day for Charlie just like today is for me."

Mr. Foster smiled. "I'm glad you're enjoying the book. Would you like to read aloud while we pick up the others?"

"Yes, sir," said Ellis Earl. He opened the book to where he had marked it with an old chewing gum wrapper he had found in a crack in the kitchen floor.

Before Ellis Earl knew it, he had read six pages, and Mr. Foster had turned the car onto a path that led to a little gray house that sat in the middle of a field. Ellis Earl stared at the house that didn't look much different from his. With the exception of a black pickup truck parked in the yard and a small room jutting out of the side of the house, everything else was the same—rickety steps leading up to a front porch, two windows on either side of the weatherworn front door, a tin roof, a chimney, and an outside toilet at the end of a well-worn path behind the house.

Ellis Earl was even more surprised when the front door opened and his friend Philip stepped out onto the porch. Philip waved and yelled, "Be right out," before going back inside.

Ellis Earl turned to Mr. Foster. "I thought Philip lived in town."

Mr. Foster's forehead creased. "No, Mr. Harris lives here with his aunt and his grandmother and a few of his cousins. Who told you he lived in town?"

"Phi—" Ellis Earl paused. Philip had lied to him, but Ellis Earl understood why. He probably would have, too, if he thought he could have gotten away with it. "No one," he said to Mr. Foster, deciding to keep this information to himself. "I just thought he lived in town with his mama and daddy."

Mr. Foster's face creased into more confusion. "Mr. Harris's parents live in Harlem."

"Harlem? Where's that?"

"In New York," said Mr. Foster. "He never told you that his parents live in New York?"

Ellis Earl shook his head. "No, sir."

"Hmmm," commented Mr. Foster. "They've lived there for years. Mr. Harris was born in Harlem, in fact. His mother brought him down here to live with his grandmother when he was seven."

"How does he get to school?" Ellis Earl asked.

"His grandmother brings him," said Mr. Foster, nodding toward the black truck parked under the lone tree in the front yard.

Ellis Earl recalled all the times Philip had bragged about his life. About living in town with his parents, grandmother, and his two sisters and one brother. About their house with the six rooms and the indoor toilet. *Well, at least he told the truth about his grandmother*, thought Ellis Earl. *He really does live in the same house with her.*

When Philip came to the car a few moments later, Ellis Earl smiled at him. It was his way of saying, *I understand*. But Philip didn't return the smile. Instead a look of embarrassment flashed across his face. As he climbed into the back seat, he barely mumbled a "Good morning."

"Mr. Brown was just reading from his book, *Charlie and the Chocolate Factory*," Mr. Foster said to Philip through the rearview mirror. "Care if he continues?"

Staring out at the barren cotton fields, Philip muttered, "Fine with me."

But as Ellis Earl began reading, Philip quickly interrupted.

"*Corridor*," he said.

"I beg your pardon," said Mr. Foster.

"The word is *corridor*," Philip said snidely. "Ellis Earl said 'cor-RIDE-or.'"

"Thank you for that correction, Mr. Harris," said Mr. Foster.

Ellis Earl continued reading. The word *corridor* appeared three more times in the next few lines. Each time Ellis Earl read it, he struggled with the pronunciation. And with each struggle, Philip felt the need to correct him.

"I know how to say the word," said Ellis Earl. "You just made me nervous. Now I can't say it right."

"It's not that hard to say," Philip grumbled.

Mr. Foster interceded. "We'll never finish the chapter, Mr. Harris, if you continue to interrupt. I'm sure Mr. Brown knows how to pronounce *corridor* by now. Sometimes it's best to just allow a person to read rather than correcting every word that he or she mispronounces. He'll eventually figure it out. Besides, there's a time and a place for everything under the sun. But this is neither the time nor the place to constantly correct your friend's pronunciation. He is entertaining us by reading."

Without another word, Philip slumped down in his seat and sulked all the way to the home of the next rider. Ellis Earl was so afraid that Philip would correct him that he stumbled over nearly every word. By the time Mr. Foster picked up the fifth boy, Ellis Earl had stopped reading. He remained silent until they reached their first stop—Belzoni—where Mr. Foster had promised them a bite to eat.

Upon exiting the car, Mr. Foster pulled Philip to the side. Ellis Earl couldn't hear what he said to him, but whatever it was caused tears to bulge in Philip's eyes. After he wiped them away, Philip rejoined the other boys, turned to Ellis Earl, and told him he was sorry for the way he had behaved.

Ellis Earl was pleased. But he also vowed he would not correct his siblings again, as he now knew how it made them feel. As Mr. Foster had said, there was a time and a place for everything, and they would eventually learn along the way, just as Ellis Earl had done.

Just then, a big black car pulled up. Ellis Earl's face brightened when he saw Cora and her two brothers scramble from the back seat.

Mr. Foster chatted with Cora's parents while his carpool of boys gathered around Cora and her brothers and regaled them with the adventures of their first out-of-town car trip.

The third car that pulled up belonged to Miss Callahan, one of the three white teachers at their school. Her car was filled with girls. Two of them were Ellis Earl's classmates—Cassandra Smith, the girl who always spoke loudly, and Betty King, the girl whose cousin had been killed in a dice game. Ellis Earl didn't know the names of the other two girls, but he recognized them as students who were in grades above him.

Together, all sixteen of them headed from the parking lot to the restaurant. When they reached the entrance, Ellis Earl and his fellow classmates paused. They all saw the sign in the window: **WE SERVE WHITES ONLY.**

"Um, Mr. Foster," said Dale. He pointed at the sign. "I don't think we supposed to go in there."

"Oh, that sign means nothing," said Cora's father. "This restaurant has been integrated. They probably forgot to take the sign out of the window."

"Integrated?" said Dale. "What that mean?"

"It means colored people can eat here," said Cassandra.

Dale continued to stare at the sign. So did Ellis Earl and the other boys. On Ellis Earl's mind was the fact that Mr. Foster said a colored man from this town was shot for helping other colored people register to vote. He hoped there wouldn't be trouble.

Ding! Ding! The bell above the door rang when Cora's father opened it. And because of that sound, people took notice. Every white face in the restaurant turned and gawked at the brood of brown faces coming through the door.

Ellis Earl suddenly felt as if he needed to throw up rather than eat.

Raw Bacon and Untoasted Bread

WEARING A POWDER BLUE waitress uniform, a white woman with dull red hair and flaming red cheeks approached Cora's father. "Can I help y'all?"

"We'd like a table, well, several tables, actually," said Mr. Scott.

Glowering, the waitress turned and scanned the restaurant. "As you can clearly see," she said, "we don't have no tables large enough to seat all y'all."

Ellis Earl exhaled with relief. What she said was true. There were empty tables, but none of them was large enough to seat sixteen people.

Cora's father laughed lightheartedly. "Ma'am, we don't all have to sit at the same table." He gestured around the restaurant. "I believe there is enough empty space scattered throughout your establishment to accommodate our party."

The waitress scowled at Cora's father. Frankly, her eyes seemed to burn a hole through the group. But when she caught a glimpse of Miss Callahan, her eyes turned stone-cold. "I'll need to speak with the boss about this," she said. Her face was so tense that her lips barely moved. "We don't usually have to *separate* parties," she said, looking directly at Miss Callahan.

Ellis Earl didn't know why the waitress had leaned forward and emphasized the word *separate*, but it made him uncomfortable. His body stiffened, and his breathing came in short gasps. He didn't feel as if he were a member of any kind of party. He felt as if he were trapped inside a very bad dream instead.

As they waited for the waitress to return, the patrons in the restaurant continued to stare. They all had plates of food—pancakes, biscuits, grits, gravy, bacon, eggs. But none of them was touching that delicious food. The sixteen people who had just entered their restaurant seemed much more interesting.

Even the colored cook, who was wearing a white uniform and white hat, stopped working at the grill to stare at them. To Ellis Earl, his eyes seemed to say, *Please, don't start trouble.*

From the back of the restaurant came the voice of the waitress screaming at the boss about the sign not working. Ellis Earl assumed she was speaking of the sign in the front window—the one that said they only served white people. When he heard the boss yell something about the law and calling it damned, Ellis Earl quivered with fear.

Miss Callahan leaned over to Mr. Foster and whispered, "Julius, are y'all sure this is the right restaurant? Maybe this isn't the one that's integrated."

Ellis Earl detected fear in her voice as well.

"We're sure," said Mr. Foster.

As soon as he said that, the waitress came storming from the back of the restaurant. She didn't look happy as she glanced around nervously at the other patrons. Still scowling, she said to Cora's father, "Y'all kin follow me."

The group was spread out among four tables that seated four people each. At Ellis Earl's table sat Ellis Earl, Philip, Cassandra, and Cora, as Cora's younger brothers sat at the table with her parents. Ellis Earl wished one of Cora's parents had sat with them instead. He would have preferred the protection of an adult over the company of a peer.

Even with them sitting right next to Mr. Foster's table, Ellis Earl couldn't control the shaking of his hands. He placed them in his lap. There wasn't much he could do about his leg except to allow his foot to tap against the tiled floor.

"Tell me some more about your book," Cora said cheerfully. Ellis Earl could tell she was only making small talk to counteract the stares from the people in the restaurant.

Ellis Earl tried to tell Cora about *Charlie and the Chocolate Factory*, but the stares soon turned to words, causing him to lose his focus.

Uppity. Negroes. Disgrace.

Though only whispers, the words soared through the air, then crashed, exploding in Ellis Earl's ears like tiny bombs.

This type of thing had never happened to him

before. He squeezed his eyes shut to keep the rush of tears from falling.

Maybe Mama was right. Maybe I shouldn't have come. She warned me about mean-spirited white people, but she thought they would only be at the airport.

Except for some of the teachers at his school, like Miss Callahan, Ellis Earl had never been around many white people. Mama had. She knew what she was talking about. He should have listened.

When some of their food finally came, the waitress slammed their plates on the tables with great exaggeration. Everyone at Ellis Earl's table seemed to let out a breath at the same time. Until they saw the food.

"Excuse me, miss," Mr. Foster called after the waitress.

She stopped and spun around on her heels. "Is there something else I can help you people with?" she asked, glaring.

"As a matter of fact, there is," said Mr. Foster. "You can bring us some food that has been properly cooked."

With eyes as evil as a snake in the Garden of

Eden, the waitress scoffed and said, "We don't cook for coloreds 'round here. Coloreds cook for *us*."

With that she gave one last accusing eye roll toward Miss Callahan, then stormed back to the kitchen. She left the RFK Welcoming Team staring at their plates of raw bacon and untoasted bread.

Silence and Sadness

THE CAR WAS COMPLETELY SILENT when Mr. Foster got back on the highway. No more chatter from the once cheerful boys who had never been out of town. No more chapters of *Charlie and the Chocolate Factory*. No more correction of Ellis Earl's pronunciation.

Just silence.

Silence and sadness.

Ellis Earl, who was now sitting in the back seat, as he had offered the front seat to Philip, rested his head against the window and stared out. He had at first been embarrassed when he could no longer control his tears and had cried in the restaurant.

But when he looked up, he saw that Cora and Philip were crying, too. By the time they reached the car, all the children were crying.

The adults, however, had some choice words that they wanted to convey to the boss, but he refused to leave the back of the restaurant. Instead he had called the police on a bunch of trouble-making Negroes from out of town.

Knowing they didn't have time to deal with that kind of nonsense, Mr. Foster and his companions rushed to their cars and fled at the sound of sirens blaring in the distance. Other than a short stop at a service station, which only Cora's parents went inside to purchase snacks and sodas for everyone, there was no more stopping for a sit-down meal.

The sleep that Ellis Earl had missed the night before suddenly came upon him about half an hour after they left the restaurant. When he awoke, it was to the sound of Dale and Jerry and Willie commenting about the height of buildings. They were in the city of Jackson.

Ellis Earl sat up and rubbed the sleep from his eyes. He was disappointed to see that he had creased his shirt when he slept with his arms folded across his chest. He hoped everyone would be too busy looking for the senator to notice the wrinkles. But he was even more disappointed that he had fallen asleep and missed most of the scenery between Belzoni and Jackson. He had even missed the city called Yazoo City. He wanted to share every detail of the trip with his siblings, especially Carrie Ann and Oscar. Mr. Foster had said it would be night when they returned. Ellis Earl would have to make do with what he could see in the dark.

But now that he was awake, and now that they were in Jackson, he pressed his face against the window to take in every detail. Stores. Restaurants. Filling stations. Banks. Office buildings. All these things clustered one after another, unlike in his little town, where everything fit on one stretch of road.

This is the kind of place where I want to live, thought Ellis Earl. *This is the kind of life I want for me and my family when I grow up.*

"It's so big," Dale whispered. "They got everything here."

"I wish I lived here," said Jerry. He pointed at an ice cream shop. "I would eat ice cream every single day."

"You gotta still have some money to buy the ice cream," said Willie.

"I bet they don't let coloreds get ice cream in there no way," said Dale.

The dark cloud that had eventually vanished along the long ride suddenly loomed again with Dale's reminder that, as colored people, they could not freely walk into any establishment they chose to and be served.

"Is Jackson segregated, too?" Willie asked Mr. Foster.

"It's not supposed to be," said Mr. Foster. "But as you just witnessed, the law means nothing to some people. They'll still find ways to serve only the ones they wish to serve."

"What about the airport?" asked Ellis Earl, remembering Mama's words. "Will we be safe there?"

"Yes," said Mr. Foster. "Everyone is welcome at the airport."

The boys continued to stare out the window but said nothing. Ellis Earl was happy to see a sign directing them to the airport. Perhaps seeing the senator would bring some joy back to them, and they could be as happy returning home as they had been when they initially left.

A collective cheer sounded in the car. The airport was in view. None of the boys had ever seen an airplane other than crop dusters. But there was one, in plain view, landing at the airport.

"A airplane! A airplane!" Dale cried.

"We can all see that," Philip said dryly.

Mr. Foster gave him a quick but stern look.

"Sorry," he muttered.

"All right, gentlemen," said Mr. Foster. "I chose the five of you because I knew you would be on your best behavior. I know that none of you will do anything to bring shame to the Negro race while at this airport. Therefore I expect you to live up to my expectations. Understood?"

"Yes, sir!" all the boys, including Philip, said eagerly.

Mr. Foster smiled. "Then let's go welcome the senator to our state."

They met the rest of their crew—Cora's family and Miss Callahan and the girls—in the parking lot. It seemed the incident at the restaurant in Belzoni was a million miles behind them and nothing lay ahead but the anticipation of seeing an important man and possibly having the opportunity to wave at him from a distance.

But something felt off for Ellis Earl. Something was not quite right. Mama's words were still nagging him.

Just then, while his intuition was speaking to him, Dale spoke to the group out loud. "How come there so many police cars out here?"

Race Mixers Go Home

"THE SENATOR IS IMPORTANT," said Philip. "He needs protection."

"He just one man," said Dale. "Shouldn't take *this* many police. Look like 'bout thirty cars out here."

Mr. Foster cleared his throat, which seemed to remind Dale to be on his best behavior.

Ellis Earl was still taking note of all the police cars when he bumped right into Dale, who had abruptly stopped walking.

The entire group, as a matter of fact, had halted.

"God, help us," whispered Cora's mother.

Ellis Earl couldn't see what they saw, but he heard the chanting. And some of the words were the same ones he'd heard at the restaurant in Belzoni.

And some were worse.

As he squeezed himself between Mr. Foster and Miss Callahan, he caught a glimpse of what the others saw: a line of white people—men, women, and children—marching back and forth and holding signs.

TO HELL WITH BOBBY K!

RACE MIXERS GO HOME!

SEND BOBBY TO HANOI, NOT MISSISSIPPI!

Dale leaned close to Ellis Earl. "Hanoi?" he whispered. "Where that at?"

Ellis Earl shrugged.

"Hanoi is the capital of Vietnam," whispered Philip. "They're talking about the war. The one that Muhammad Ali might go to jail for 'cause he won't go fight in it."

"You mean Cassius Clay?" whispered Betty.

"No. I mean Muhammad Ali," said Philip.

Ellis Earl had heard talk about the war in Vietnam. And he had heard his brothers say that

Muhammad Ali was going to jail because he wouldn't fight in it. But that was all he knew. He wondered what that had to do with Robert Kennedy coming to Mississippi to talk about how to help poor people live better.

"That's a tough crowd to walk through," Cora's father said dryly.

"But if we want to see the senator, then we have no choice," said his wife.

"We didn't come this far to turn around," said Mr. Foster.

"Amen," said Miss Callahan.

Bravely they all raised their heads and walked toward the menacing group of protesters. Ellis Earl could tell that they were doing their best to shield Miss Callahan from being seen by the protesters.

Ellis Earl's legs felt like jelly, but he managed to move them forward, one step at a time. Mr. Foster had told them to keep their chins up—don't look down at the sidewalk, but don't look at the protesters either. But the minute they reached the protesters, one of them yelled out, "Well, would you look at that! A bunch of monkeys come from Africa to see that darky lover get off the plane!"

The other protesters hooted and hollered.

"Ignore them and keep walking," said Mr. Foster.

"We're gonna send Bobby K. back to Washington in a pine box!" a protester yelled. "Any of you coons wanna join him?"

Ellis Earl noticed that Philip's hands were clenched into fists, his face pinched tight. "Just keep walking," Ellis Earl whispered to him.

But Philip didn't keep walking. Instead he stopped and stared at the protesters.

"Ain't gonna let nobody turn me around," he sang softly. *"Turn me around, turn me around. Ain't gonna let nobody turn me around. I'm gonna keep on a-walkin', keep on a-talkin', marchin' up to freedom land."*

When Mr. Foster stepped toward Philip to stop him, Miss Callahan touched his arm. She shook her head. Mr. Foster nodded and stepped back.

Philip raised his voice, and Ellis Earl joined him. *"Ain't gonna let segregation turn me around. Turn me around, turn me around. Ain't gonna let segregation turn me around. I'm gonna keep on a-walkin', keep on a-talkin', marchin' up to freedom land."*

One by one, the other children joined in as they sang, *"Ain't gonna let Mississippi turn me around.*

Turn me around, turn me around. Ain't gonna let Mississippi turn me around. I'm gonna keep on a-walkin', keep on a-talkin', marchin' up to freedom land."

With the protesters sufficiently silenced, the RFK Welcoming Team marched on.

The Lucky Ones

THEY ALL SEEMED TO RELEASE a collective sigh when they finally made it out of shouting distance from the protesters.

"Is everyone okay?" asked Mr. Foster once they were safely inside the airport.

Along with everyone else, Ellis Earl nodded that he was okay. But his insides were all jumbled up. His stomach ached. Did that crowd of people really intend to send Mr. Kennedy home in a pine box? What if he was assassinated like his brother? What if it happened right here at the airport?

Ellis Earl uttered a quick prayer for the senator's safety as well as his own.

Mr. Foster glanced at his watch. "Despite the delays, looks like we made it just in time," he said. "The senator's plane should be arriving soon."

"Will we really get to see him?" asked Cassandra.

Mr. Foster pointed. "Right through those glass doors is where he'll come." He smiled. "We'll all see him. Might even get to shake his hand if we're lucky."

Ellis Earl tapped his foot anxiously. What should have been a glorious moment had been tainted by both the incident in Belzoni and the protesters outside the airport. He scanned the crowd. Besides them, there were only a few other colored people at the airport. This made him feel uncomfortable.

Philip seemed to notice. He touched Ellis Earl's shoulder and beckoned him out of earshot from the rest of the group.

"Thanks for helping me out with the song," he said.

Ellis Earl took a deep breath to calm himself. He didn't want his voice to falter when he spoke. "That was brave. I could never do what you just did."

"You joined in," said Philip. "That was brave enough."

Ellis Earl smiled but remained silent. No one had ever called him brave.

"I know I said I was sorry earlier," Philip said, "but I'm saying it again. This time from my heart and of my own accord, not because Mr. Foster told me to. He's right. There's enough fighting going on in the world already. We saw that today. We shouldn't be fighting each other."

Ellis Earl's smile widened. This was exactly what Mama had said to him and Carrie Ann. *Enough fighting going on in the world already without y'all adding to it.*

"I'm sorry, too," he told Philip. "You're right. I'm jealous because you know so much about everything Mr. Foster talks about in class. And because you read those Hardy Boys books."

Philip bit his bottom lip, and Ellis Earl worried that he had angered him. "I—" Philip began, but then stopped and lowered his gaze to the floor.

"I'm really, *really* sorry," said Ellis Earl.

After a moment that felt uncomfortably long to Ellis Earl, Philip looked up. Tears brimmed his eyes. "I was jealous of you, too."

"Of me?" Ellis Earl forced himself not to smile. Smiling would be a rude thing to do. But the thought of Philip Harris being even slightly jealous of him made his heart sing.

"I was jealous because you have a big family," Philip said.

Ellis Earl couldn't imagine anyone, especially Philip, being jealous of his large family. Why would anyone want to be surrounded by so many people in such a small space? Ellis Earl loved them, sure. But if given a choice, he'd take a couple of siblings and be done with it.

"I . . ." Philip paused and bit his lip again. "I don't have any sisters and brothers," he said quickly. "Just cousins. And they're not very nice to me."

He sucked in a breath as if fighting back tears. "They don't like me because my mama sends me packages. And my daddy writes me these boring poems. My parents live in New York. The only thing I ever get from them are the packages, mainly books and a set of new clothes—four pairs of pants and four shirts—when school starts, then another set at Christmastime. I can't remember the last time they came to see me." He muttered the last sentence so quietly that Ellis Earl barely heard him.

"I'm really, *really* sorry," Ellis Earl said again. He didn't know what else to say to comfort his friend.

They stood silently for a moment, staring at the floor. Ellis Earl felt bad for having been jealous of Philip, thinking he was lucky because he had a few nice clothes. He remembered something that his uncle Joseph had said once about his own children when Ellis Earl said they were lucky they got everything they wanted. "Children who get everything they want ain't always the lucky ones," Uncle Joseph had said.

Philip had clothes from his parents. He had packages and poems from his parents. But he didn't have his parents. Philip wasn't lucky at all.

"Have you ever asked your parents if you can go live with them?" Ellis Earl asked.

Philip shrugged. "I used to. But I got tired of the same old answer. Got tired of them saying they had to take care of some things first. So I stopped asking."

"Maybe start small," said Ellis Earl. "Maybe ask them if you can visit for a week this summer."

"I could try that. They used to worry that I couldn't stay by myself while they worked. But I'm twelve now. I'm old enough to take care of myself."

Philip smiled. "That's what I'll do. I'll write them and ask if I can visit for a week."

"Everything okay, Mr. Harris and Mr. Brown?" So lost in their conversation, Ellis Earl and Philip hadn't noticed Mr. Foster's presence.

Ellis Earl gave Mr. Foster a smile. "Everything is great," he said.

Mr. Foster left them alone and rejoined the group.

"I'd like to read your book when you're done with it," Philip said.

"It's got pictures in it," warned Ellis Earl.

Philip shrugged. "That's okay. I'd still like to read it."

Smiling, the two boys joined the others and waited with the crowd for Senator Robert Kennedy's arrival. Before they knew it, the people in the airport suddenly began cheering.

"He's coming!" said Cora.

In that moment, everything that had plagued Ellis Earl faded away like a dream that one struggled hard to remember but simply couldn't. The senator was here, and he was about to come through the glass doors where Mr. Foster had pointed.

Ellis Earl's breath caught in his throat. Was this really happening to an insignificant little boy such as himself?

The noise of the crowd grew louder, and people began pressing toward the doors through which the senator would enter. Newspaper crews with cameras hanging about their necks waited in position, cameras poised to get the first shots.

Click. Click. Click. Click. Click. The cameras flashed. And the noise of the crowd exploded. Ellis Earl's heart thumped wildly as he stretched up on his toes and craned his neck.

Then the doors opened.

Click. Click. Click. Click. Click.

Flash! Flash! Flash! Flash! Flash!

Through the doors walked a man with a smile draping his face.

Hands stretched out to him. He reached out and shook them from both sides, using his right hand and his left.

Ellis Earl thought his heart would explode as the man slowly made his way through the crowd, reaching out to all the hands extended toward him. When he got close, Ellis Earl reached out his hand, too. He didn't know whether his was one of the hands the senator would touch, but he at least wanted to try.

The senator was coming down the line. He was right in front of Ellis Earl. His hand was outstretched toward Ellis Earl's—

But it missed him by a hair, grabbing and vigorously shaking Philip's hand instead.

Yo' Blues Ain't Like Mines

ELLIS EARL HAD EXPECTED most of his family would be in bed by the time Mr. Foster took him home. But the yellow glow of the kerosene lamp showing through the front windows told him otherwise. And Ellis Earl could see that someone was peering out the window when Mr. Foster's car pulled into the yard.

Being the first one picked up on the way to Jackson, he was also the last to be dropped off. And as he had done with each of the other boys, Mr. Foster parked his car in order to walk Ellis Earl to the door and thank his mother for allowing him to take the trip. He also wanted to check on Oscar.

Even though Ellis Earl was slightly disappointed that the senator had bypassed his hand and shaken Philip's, he was still elated from the day's adventure, despite the incident at the restaurant in Belzoni. On the way back, at least, they had stopped at a Negro-owned restaurant and had enjoyed a delicious meal without incident.

When they had arrived at the restaurant, Dale, known for his brashness, spoke aloud what Ellis Earl had been considering silently. "They gon' let Miss Callahan eat here?" Dale had asked Mr. Foster. "I know the sign say 'Miss Rita's Soul Food Restaurant: Everybody Welcome,' but do that mean Miss Callahan, too?"

"Of course it means Miss Callahan," Mr. Foster had said. "Colored restaurants have always been integrated. All have always been welcome. Now, let's go eat some soul food."

And that's exactly what they had done. Ellis Earl's belly was still full, so full, in fact, that he felt as if that one meal of chicken, collard greens, cornbread, candied yams, macaroni and cheese, banana pudding, peach cobbler, and pound cake would last him three days.

The front door opened the second Ellis Earl

put one foot on the porch. He expected Mama, but instead it was Oscar who opened the door.

"Earl back, y'all!" he called over his shoulder to the rest of the family. "Did you see him? Did you see him? Did you see Mr. Robert Kennedy?"

Ellis Earl was so stunned to see Oscar standing at the door that he couldn't speak.

"Did you see him?" Oscar asked again. He leaned against the door frame and tilted his head to one side.

"I, um," stumbled Ellis Earl. "Um, yeah. I saw Mr. Robert Kennedy."

"Well, ain't you excited?" asked Oscar.

"I'm . . ." Ellis Earl tilted his own head to one side and studied his brother. "How come you ain't laying down?"

Oscar smiled. "'Cause I been waitin' for you. I wanted to make sho' I was still woke when you got home, so I been sittin' up this whole time."

"You ain't tired?" asked Ellis Earl.

"A lil' bit," said Oscar. "But seeing you is makin' me feel a whole lot better."

"Wow. You got up just like Grandpa Joe did when Charlie found that golden ticket."

Oscar beamed. "Yep! I sho' did!"

Ellis Earl stopped in the doorway and hugged his brother. He held him close for a moment before they entered the house.

"Did you see Mr. Robert Kennedy up close?" Oscar asked. "Or was he far away?"

"I saw him up close!" said Ellis Earl. "I almost shook his hand!"

Oscar let out a whistle. "Whew, boy. That musta been something."

Ellis Earl beamed. "It *was* something. It was everything. He shook my friend Philip's hand, and that was good enough for me."

"And thanks for the doughnut," said Oscar. "That was the best birthday surprise ever!" He grabbed Ellis Earl in a hug again and said, "I missed you, big brother!"

After having been with Mr. Foster, and his friends, and Cora and her family, and Miss Callahan, and the girls, and seeing cities, and going to an airport, and seeing a United States senator, and almost shaking his hand, Ellis Earl felt as if he had stepped into another world when he stepped inside the rundown shack he called home. Yes, he missed his family, especially after his conversation with Philip. But now that he had seen another side of life, he knew that he would find it even harder to be content with the one he had. Yet he had no choice for the moment, so he would concentrate on doing his best in school so that he could one day create the life he wanted to live.

He said to Oscar, "I missed you, too, little brother."

He hugged Mama, who was standing behind Oscar. "I missed you, too, Mama."

"Boy, you ain't gotta act like you been gone a week," Mama said, squeezing him tight.

Mr. Foster, who still stood at the door since he had not been invited inside, chuckled.

"Oh, Mr. Foster, where my manners?" asked Mama. "Would you like to come in and set for a spell?"

With a gentle smile, Mr. Foster replied, "I appreciate the offer, Mrs. Brown, but I just wanted to walk Ellis to the door and to see how Oscar is doing. I see he's doing fine," he said, nodding. "But I really must be going. School tomorrow."

"Well, I sho' do 'ppreciate what you did for Earl today," Mama said. "I know he ain't gon' never forget this."

"It was my plea—" Mr. Foster paused and

poked his head in the doorway. He tilted his ear toward the middle room. "Mr. Brown?" he said to Ellis Earl, "Is that your sister I hear singing?"

Mama waved her hand. "Oh, don't mind them, Mr. Foster. They been doin' this later and later every night now, keeping me and the girls from going to bed. They take they work real serious and been spending as much time as they kin to practice for that talent show."

At the words *talent show*, Ellis Earl cringed.

"On second thought," said Mr. Foster, "perhaps I will sit for a spell. I'd like to listen to them for a bit."

When Mama motioned Mr. Foster inside, Ellis Earl bit his lip. *Please don't say another word about that talent show*, he willed everyone in the house.

"Yo' blues ain't like mines," Jeannette sang.

> *Nah, nah, baby.*
> *I got my blues. You got yo' blues.*
> *But yo' blues still ain't like mines.*

Ellis Earl noticed Mr. Foster's smile and the tapping of his foot.

The blues ain't red, baby,
And the blues ain't pank.
The blues ain't even yellow, honey,
But the blues sho' stank.

This time when Jeannette said "pank," Ellis Earl did not have the urge to cry out, "Pink!" *Pank* rhymed with *stank*, and *stank* was all right in Ellis Earl's book, because the blues didn't stink. The blues stank.

Mr. Foster sat and listened to the Brown Blues rehearse two more songs before he turned to Mama and said, "Your children sing beautifully, Mrs. Brown. Like professionals. I'm glad they'll be performing in the talent show next Sunday, but I think they should be heard by someone in the music business as well."

Surprise lit up Mama's face. "Oh," was all she managed to say.

"A member of our church has connections with a record studio in Memphis," Mr. Foster continued. "He might be able to get the Brown Blues some studio time."

"Oh, my," Mama said quietly.

"I told y'all!" Deidra said, her eyes wide. "I told y'all they was gon' be on the radio one day!"

"Wow," Ellis Earl said, letting out a breath. "They said they wanted to be like B. B. King."

"Don't go puttin' the cart 'foe the horse now," Mama warned her children. "They ain't never sung in front of nobody but us. Let 'em sang in the talent show first. See how they do."

"Yeah!" cried Carrie Ann. "Let 'em sang in the talent show so they can win all that money!"

Ellis Earl sucked in his breath again. He wished he could suck in Carrie Ann's words, too, to keep them from reaching Mr. Foster's ears.

"They ain't just doing it for the money, Carr'Ann," Mama said. "They singing 'cause they want to."

Carrie Ann shook her head. "Nuh-uh. I heard Andre tell Jeannette, 'We need to do this. We need that money.'"

Looking confused, Mr. Foster said, "Mr. Brown, is there something you would like to explain to me?"

Without raising his head, Ellis Earl muttered, "I told them that the winner of the talent show got a bucket of money."

"That ain't the truth?" Mama asked Mr. Foster.

"I'm afraid not, Mrs. Brown. There is . . ." He sighed and shook his head at Ellis Earl. "There is no monetary prize attached to our talent shows. The shows are simply a fun way for the youth to express themselves. It's more for fellowship than anything. I'm sorry that Ellis made it more serious than it is."

He said to Ellis Earl, "Mr. Brown, I'm disappointed."

Tears began streaming down Ellis Earl's face. "I just wanted everybody to go to church. I didn't mean to lie. It just happened. Then I wanted to tell the truth. I wanted to fix it. But all this other stuff happened like going to the airport, and I just—I just—I didn't know what to do."

They all silently stared at him for a moment.

"Ooo-weee, Earl!" cried Carrie Ann. "They gon' git you for telling that big ol' story!"

"Carr'Ann, stop it!" Mama chastised. She turned to Ellis Earl. "Earl, you have to make this right."

Ellis Earl nodded and wiped his face. "I know."

Mama addressed Mr. Foster. "Earl been wanting us all to go to church ever since you took him for Easter. He didn't mean no harm, Mr. Foster. He really enjoyed himself and wanted the rest of 'em to know that feeling, too."

"I think that's a wonderful idea, Mrs. Brown. Your family should indeed come to church, regardless of whether your older children perform in the talent show or not. But . . . they are extremely talented, and there's no point in letting all that talent go to waste. I'm absolutely sure that my friend would be interested in hearing them sing. I can arrange a time for him to hear them outside of church."

"My brothers don't like church no ways," Carrie Ann said.

"That's what I thought, too," said Ellis Earl. "Until I went."

"Truthfully, Mr. Foster," said Mama, "we really don't have nothing to wear. I was gon' let the older children and Earl go with you on Sunday, but me and all the little ones was gon' stay at the house."

"If Earl go, I'm going," Carrie Ann said, pouting and pointing at her chest.

Mr. Foster smiled at Carrie Ann, then said to Mama, "Come as you are, Mrs. Brown. All are welcome. Fancy clothes or not. Ellis, Carrie Ann, and Oscar have always been neatly dressed when they come to school. That's all that matters, Mrs. Brown."

"I don't mean to disrespect you, Mr. Foster," Mama said. "But if that be the truth, then how come you bought my boy new clothes 'foe he went to yo' church?"

"I'm sorry if I sent the wrong message, Mrs. Brown. I bought Ellis Earl a new outfit because one of the other young men asked me if I would get him a new outfit. If one was going to have a new outfit, I thought it was only proper that they all had one so that he wouldn't stand out."

"Whew, boy!" said Oscar. "You must be rich!"

Mr. Foster chuckled. "Quite the contrary, Mr. Brown. I'm the one who shopped for the outfits and delivered them. But several of my friends and I pooled our money to pay for them."

"You sho' we don't need to dress up?" Mama asked.

"I'm absolutely sure," said Mr. Foster. "Please, Mrs. Brown, come as you are. Plenty of people do."

"How we all gon' get there?" asked Mama.

"I can make two trips out," said Mr. Foster.

"Uncle Joseph can take some of us," said Ellis

Earl. "The little ones will be gone home by then, so there'll be enough room for you, Carrie Ann, Beatrice, and Deidra."

"What about Oscar?" asked Mama. "Where he supposed to be while everybody gone to church?"

"I can go to church, too," said Oscar. "I'm feeling better. See?" He flexed his puny arm muscles.

Mr. Foster laughed. "Looks like you're out of excuses, Mrs. Brown," he said, smiling warmly at Mama. "I would *love* to have the entire Brown family as my honored guests on Sunday. Shall I swing by around nine thirty to pick up Ellis and the Brown Blues?"

"Please, Mama," said Ellis Earl. "You know Uncle Joseph will pick you up if you get word to him."

Mama glanced toward the middle room, where Jeannette, Andre, Aaron, and Raymond continued to sing. "Go on in there and make things right with your brothers and your sister," she told Ellis Earl. "I'll get word to Joe to give us a ride. We'll all go to church on Sunday, the older ones, too—just this one time, whether they want to or not. And if they don't like it, I won't make 'em go again."

"Yay!" all the children cried. As they pumped

their fists in the air and danced around the room, Ellis Earl no longer regretted telling a half-truth to the Brown Blues. At least now his entire family would be attending church, even if for only one Sunday.

"Mr. Foster," he said as he headed to the middle room, "you can pick me and Carrie Ann up in front of the house in the morning."

"Thank the good Lord!" Carrie Ann cried.

Mr. Foster smiled. "It will be my pleasure, Mr. Brown."

TUESDAY, APRIL 11

A Mighty Fine Boy

ELLIS EARL HADN'T WANTED to tell Mama about the sore throat because he didn't want to miss school. But the loud, body-shaking cough was something that he could not hide. So there he lay on the mattress feeling miserable and heartbroken because he couldn't go to school for the second day in a row. He couldn't believe he had missed Monday. He could only imagine the conversation among his classmates regarding their trip to the airport.

It seemed it had been a full day since Mr. Foster's station wagon pulled into the yard and only Carrie Ann had raced out to the porch, bounded down the steps, hopped into the back seat, and headed off to school. But it had only been four hours, and Ellis Earl had slept away most of them.

Monday had been worse.

It seemed the stronger Oscar got, the weaker Ellis Earl became. Would Oscar be replacing him in the carpool the way Larry had replaced Oscar in January? Ellis Earl sure hoped not. He didn't know how he would manage if he couldn't go to school for the rest of April and most of May. It would be nice if Oscar were well enough to finish out the school year, but Ellis Earl wanted to finish it, too.

"Too much been happening with you, Earl," Mama had told him before she left the house that morning. "Calm down and get some rest. You'll get better soon."

He sure hoped so. There was no way he wanted to miss church on Sunday, especially since the Brown Blues had decided to perform in the talent show even if there was no prize money. *And* Ellis Earl was pretty sure they'd win.

The scent of bread baking—biscuits, to be exact—had awakened him. His sore throat hindered him from desiring food, but he was happy that the little ones would have something to eat. He was also happy to see that Oscar was sitting in one of the rocking chairs. He was surrounded by the little children. He was reading *Charlie and the Chocolate Factory* to them.

"Hey, you woke!" Oscar said when he noticed Ellis Earl staring at them. "I kin come over there and read to you if you want."

"I'd like that," said Ellis Earl.

So Oscar and all the little ones moved their story time to the mattress and sat there with Ellis Earl.

Oscar handed him the book. "Here. You wanna read it?"

Ellis Earl shook his head. His throat was too achy, and his head was too throbby. "I'll just listen to you."

Though Oscar hadn't been keeping up with his studies, in Ellis Earl's opinion, he read beautifully. It wouldn't take much for him to catch up if he was able to go to school soon.

Beautiful reading or not, it wasn't long before Ellis Earl had dozed off again, and the next time he woke, it was to the sound of a car pulling into the yard. He raised his head. "Carrie Ann back?" he asked groggily.

"It's too early," said Oscar. "School ain't out

yet." He had long since put the book away and now sat on the floor playing a card game with the little ones.

"Maybe our daddy came to get us today," said Jewel.

"That ain't yo' daddy's car," said Jeannette. "It run too good. Yo' daddy ain't coming till Friday no how."

Oscar got up from the floor. "I'll see who it is." Peering through the window, he frowned. "It's some white people."

"*White* people?" said Jeannette. "They gettin' out?"

"Uh-huh," said Oscar. "And coming to the house."

"Comin—" Jeannette raced to the window. "Lord," she whispered. "What these white people want?"

Ellis Earl, hearing footsteps on the porch, wanted to get up and look, too. But before he had time to rise from the mattress, there was a gentle knock at the door.

Jeannette opened it. A white man stood on the other side. Behind him stood others, including a man with a fancy camera—just like what Ellis Earl had seen at the airport. Ellis Earl wondered . . . Mr. Foster's words came floating back to him: *Perhaps Senator Kennedy will take a moment to visit the Delta. Perhaps yours will be the lucky home he'll visit.* Ellis Earl shook his head and thought, *No way.*

"Good afternoon," the man said.

"Good afternoon," parroted Jeannette. There was a tremble in her voice.

"Are you the woman of the house?" the man asked.

Jeannette looked suspiciously at the crowd of strangers. "My mama ain't here right now."

"I'm Senator Robert Kennedy," the man said. "Would it be okay for us to come inside for a few moments and ask you some questions?"

At the name Kennedy, all the children in the Brown household who were old enough to reason let out a gasp. Especially Ellis Earl.

Suddenly his throat didn't feel as achy, nor was his head as throbby. Was he still asleep and dreaming? How could this be possible? How could Senator Robert Kennedy be at his house? *Why* would he be at his house?

"Y'all ain't takin' our pictures, is you?" Jeannette asked Senator Kennedy.

"We don't have to take pictures, if that's what you prefer."

Jeannette glanced back at the children, then shook her head. "I don't want our pictures took."

Senator Kennedy motioned the man with the camera to stay outside.

When Senator Kennedy entered the house, followed by several others, including a colored woman, Ellis Earl sprang up to a sitting position on the mattress. He didn't want to appear lazy to these people. But as he looked around the room—at the two broken-down chairs, at the two lard buckets turned upside down and draped with towels to serve as tables, at the mattress where he and Oscar and Lil' Walt and Prince for the past month had slept, at the wood heater, at the sparseness and simplicity of the room, at their poverty—shame still swallowed him.

One of the senator's crew extended his hand to Jeannette. "I'm Peter Edelman. It's a pleasure to meet you."

Jeannette hesitantly shook the man's hand. "My name Jeannette Brown." She didn't tell the man that it was a pleasure to meet him, although Ellis

Earl thought she should have. It would have been the polite thing to do.

The colored woman standing next to the man named Peter Edelman extended her hand to Jeannette. "And I'm Marian Wright. It's nice to meet you, Jeannette."

Jeannette shook the woman's hand. "Nice to meet you."

Ellis Earl startled. *Did that woman say her name was Marian Wright? Couldn't have. Miss Marian Wright is the lady lawyer. She wouldn't be at my house. But . . . if Senator Robert Kennedy is here, then it's possible that Miss Marian Wright could be, too.*

Ellis Earl thought that surely he was running a fever and that it was causing him to see and hear things that weren't real. This time, he did pinch himself. And that pinch was as real as the sore throat that he had had since late Sunday night. He was not dreaming.

A man who had been scribbling on a notepad since he entered the house glanced up momentarily and asked, "How many people live here?"

Jeannette's forehead creased as if she had to do a mental count. "Eleven," she said.

The man with the notepad looked confused. Anyone could see by a quick scan of the room that there were already nearly that many children present.

Jeannette gestured toward the nieces and nephews. “Them my brother’s children. They don’t live here. They going home Friday.”

“Are you here alone with all these children?” asked Miss Wright.

“Yes, ma’am,” Jeannette answered. “I always take care of the children while Mama ’n ’em work.”

“Your mother and father?” the senator asked, his brows raised.

Jeannette answered, “My mama and my three brothers.”

“What kind of work do they do?” asked the senator.

Jeannette shrugged. “Whatever kind of work they kin find.”

“How old are you?” Miss Wright asked.

“Fourteen,” answered Jeannette.

Miss Wright glanced around the room. “You have a huge responsibility for someone your age. You don’t go to school?”

“No, ma’am.”

The senator gestured around the room. "Do any of the children go to school?"

Ellis Earl scrambled to his feet. "I do. But I'm sick today, so I couldn't go."

"What ails you?" the senator asked.

"Just a cold, I think," said Ellis Earl.

The senator walked over to him and placed his hand on Ellis Earl's forehead. "At least there's no fever. So that's a good thing."

"I saw you," Ellis Earl said.

"Beg your pardon?" said the senator.

"I saw you at the airport on Sunday."

The senator's forehead crinkled. "How did you see me at the airport on Sunday?" He glanced around. There was obviously no television in the room.

"I was at the airport. I went with my teacher and some other folks from my school," said Ellis Earl. "You almost shook my hand. But Philip got in front of me. And you shook his hand."

The senator grinned broadly. "Is that so?"

Ellis Earl nodded. "Yes, sir."

"What's your name?"

"Ellis Earl."

"That's a mighty fine name," said the senator.

"You share a name with a famous place in New York called Ellis Island. Did you know that?"

"No, sir," Ellis Earl answered. A smile spread across his face. He couldn't believe he had the same name as a famous island.

"A mighty fine name for a mighty fine boy," the senator said, stretching out his hand to shake Ellis Earl's. "Nice to meet you, Ellis Earl."

After shaking the senator's hand, Ellis Earl felt dizzy from the excitement. He had to sit back on the mattress to calm himself.

"How did you find our house way out here?" Oscar asked.

With a slight chuckle, Senator Robert Kennedy replied, "Would you believe a cat led the way? We were passing through, and there he was, right in the middle of the road."

"Lucky!" said Oscar.

"Yes, he is," replied Senator Kennedy. "I'm glad we didn't hit him."

"No, Lucky is our cat," said Ellis Earl. "He sometimes likes to wander down the road, back to where we found him."

Senator Kennedy laughed. "Oh, I see."

"Senator Kennedy wanted to take a tour of the

Delta," said Miss Wright. "We've been to Cleveland, in town, to East Side. But he wanted to come out to the country, to see the rural area as well. So we brought him out here, to Wilsonville."

"Whatcha got cooking, Jeannette?" the senator asked, raising his nose in the air.

"Biscuits," said Jeannette.

"Biscuits and what?"

"Molasses."

"I mean, what else will you eat with the biscuits?"

Jeannette shrugged. "Just molasses. We ain't got nothing else to eat wit' 'em."

"What about supper?"

Jeannette lowered her head slightly and gazed at the floor. "We havin' rice," she said quietly. "We outta beans."

"Does your mother participate in the food stamp program?" asked Miss Wright.

"No, ma'am," said Jeannette, glancing up at Miss Wright. "We don't get no food stamps."

Ellis Earl remembered something Mama often said: *If you work, you eat.*

She was working.

Andre was working.

Aaron was working.

Raymond was working.

At least, they were trying to anyway. Yet their family was barely eating.

"How do you get food stamps?" he asked Miss Wright.

Jeannette glared at Ellis Earl, willing her eyes to silence him.

But he ignored her.

"Mama said she tried a few times already and couldn't get any because you have to pay to get them," he told Miss Wright.

"I'll see what I can do, Ellis Earl," said Miss Wright. "I'll do my best to help your mama get some food stamps."

For a moment, Ellis Earl thought he might cry. But he didn't. Instead he bravely asked, "Are you really Miss Marian Wright, the lawyer who went to Washington, DC?"

Miss Wright smiled warmly. "How do you know who I am?"

"My teacher, Mr. Foster, told me about you. He said you went to Washington, DC, and told the senators that people in Mississippi need food."

"I did," said Miss Wright. She nodded toward the senator. "And Senator Kennedy came to see for himself."

"Thank you," Ellis Earl said to Miss Wright and Senator Kennedy.

"You're welcome, Ellis Earl," they both replied.

"Mr. Senator Robert Kennedy," said Ellis Earl. "In school I learned that President Lyndon B. Johnson was planning on passing a law to get everybody fair housing by 1969."

The senator nodded. "That's correct. The president is trying to ensure that no one is discriminated against when it comes to housing."

"When you get back to Washington, DC, do you mind telling the president about our house so he can make sure we get one of those fair houses in 1969? As you can see . . ." He paused and glanced glumly around the front room. "We don't have much of a house at all right now. And my friend Philip—his house ain't much better. And Cassandra, a girl in my class at school, said her house only has two rooms."

The senator rubbed his chin for a moment. "I'm afraid you might be a little confused about the Fair Housing Act, Ellis. The Fair Housing Act won't be a program where houses are given away. It's a bill that ensures no one can be kept from buying or renting a home based on their race or their gender or even their religion."

Ellis Earl's shoulders slumped. "Oh," he said quietly.

"But," the senator said, smiling, "I will certainly tell the president about you and your friends. As a matter of fact, I'll make sure this entire country knows how badly families need decent housing and adequate food down here in Mississippi. And I'll do my best to make sure something is done about it, even if that means running for president myself in the next election."

A smile brightened Ellis Earl's face. "Wow. Thank you, sir." He paused for a moment, and then asked, "Are you also a lawyer, Mr. Senator?"

Senator Kennedy's brow furrowed, but he flashed another smile. "Yes, I am. Why do you ask?"

Ellis Earl looked from the senator to Miss Wright. "I'm gonna be a lawyer one day and help people the way you both do."

Miss Wright nodded. "I can certainly see that happening. You're a very smart boy, Ellis Earl. And so very caring. You'll make a fine lawyer someday."

Ellis Earl felt as if he would burst with joy.

The senator and his entourage visited the Brown home for only a few minutes, but to Ellis Earl it felt like a lifetime. He hoped that his cold symptoms would disappear overnight so that he could go to school the next morning. He couldn't wait to tell Mr. Foster that he had been right when he said perhaps the senator would visit someone's home. Perhaps someone in his class would be so lucky. Ellis Earl was thrilled beyond joy that he got to be the lucky one.

EPILOGUE

FRIDAY, MAY 12

That Old House

"THANK YOU, MR. FOSTER!"

Ellis Earl climbed from the back seat of the lime-green station wagon and waved goodbye to Mr. Foster and the other carpoolers. "See you at church on Sunday."

"You sure you don't want a ride to the house, Mr. Brown?"

"Yes, sir!" both Ellis Earl and Oscar said back.

"We wanna walk today!" said Oscar. "This one last time!"

But Carrie Ann remained glued to her spot on

the back seat. “I don’t wanna walk,” she said. “I wanna ride all the way to the house like we been doing.”

Ellis Earl reached into the car and gently tugged her arm. “Come on, little sister. You’re holding everybody up.”

“You need to exercise anyway,” said Oscar. “It’s good for you.”

Mr. Foster turned in his seat and smiled at Carrie Ann. “You’re outnumbered, Miss Brown. See you at church on Sunday.”

Carrie Ann groaned as she scooted out of the car. Reluctantly she tagged along behind her brothers. “Y’all mean,” she grumbled.

“This is our last day riding with Mr. Foster,” said Ellis Earl. “Let’s walk for old time’s sake.”

“Yeah, sis,” Oscar said. He glanced up at the sky. “It’s pretty out. It’s a good day for walking.”

“Race you to the house,” Ellis Earl said to him.

Without bothering to answer, Oscar broke into a run. Ellis Earl chased him, but he knew he’d never catch him now that Oscar had a head start.

“Hey! Wait for me!” cried Carrie Ann.

By the time the siblings reached the house, they were all out of breath. But they didn’t care.

There was too much to look forward to today—like moving.

"Wonder what time Uncle Joseph gon' git here," said Oscar as he climbed the steps. "I'm ready to go."

"He gotta get off work first," said Ellis Earl. "Mama said to just make sure we have all our stuff ready when he gets here."

Carrie Ann scoffed. "What stuff? We ain't got nothing."

Ellis Earl shrugged. "You know, anything at this house that you wanna take with you. Mama don't want you to leave something, then start complaining about it when we get to the new house."

"Ain't nothing at this ol' house that I wanna keep 'cept Lucky, and I'ma make sho' I put him in the car with me," said Carrie Ann.

"Good luck with that," said Oscar. "Uncle Joseph don't like cats."

"Just be ready when he gets here," said Ellis Earl.

"I *been* ready!" said Oscar. "I been ready ever since Deacon Burton gave Mama his house. Them sho' is some nice folks at Mr. Foster's church."

"*Our* church," corrected Ellis Earl. "We're members now."

"Humph," said Carrie Ann. "You wouldn't be calling 'em nice if you was in that mean lady's Sunday school class."

Opening the front door, Oscar said to his little sister, "Will you please stop all that complaining and just be thankful that we 'bout to move out this raggedy ol' house?"

"At least you and Beatrice and Deidra get to have a room all by yourselves," said Ellis Earl.

"And you and me ain't got to sleep on a mattress in the front room no mo'," Oscar said as he draped his arm over Ellis Earl's shoulders.

The moment they entered the house, Vera ran to Ellis Earl. She waved his much-loved copy of *Charlie and the Chocolate Factory* in the air. Philip had just returned it the day before. Ellis Earl had offered to let him keep it, take it with him when he left in two weeks to visit his parents. But Philip assured him he'd have plenty of books to read at his parents' apartment in Harlem, where he was going not just for one week, as Ellis Earl had suggested, but for the entire summer. With a little luck, maybe he would even convince them to let him finally come live with them. Ellis Earl smiled at the thought of his friend living in a big city like New York. He thought it fit Philip perfectly.

"Earl! Earl! I kin read this now," Vera said, still waving the book at him.

Ellis Earl placed his sack of end-of-school-year items on the floor and scooped Vera up in his arms. "Carrie Ann ain't the only one needing some exercise," he said. "You picking up a little weight, niece. Next thing you know, you'll be running races with us."

When Ellis Earl put her down, she showed him the book again. "I kin read this!"

"You can't read that book yet, Vera," he said, chuckling. "It's too hard for you."

"No, it ain't," she said. "I'll show you."

They both sat on the floor, and Vera opened the book to a random page. She read, "'Good-by' . . ." then stopped. She showed the book to Ellis Earl. "What's the next word?"

"Ha! Told you you couldn't read it." Ellis Earl reached for the book.

Vera snatched it back and wouldn't let him have it. "I *kin* read it. I just don't know this one word. Now tell me," she demanded.

Ellis Earl sighed. "'Violet.'"

Vera grinned. She began reading again: "'Good-by Violet. "This'" . . ." She paused, but this time she didn't ask Ellis Earl for help. She sounded out the word: "*G-u-m*. Gum!"

She started all over: "'Good-by Violet. "This gum," Mr.' . . ."

She paused and showed Ellis Earl the page. "What's the next word?"

"You should know that, Vera. I've read this to you before."

"I forgot," Vera said sheepishly.

"'Wonka,'" said Ellis Earl, smiling. He smiled not because he was satisfied that he was right about his three-year-old niece's inability to read the book. He smiled because he was proud of her for trying. "Mr. Willy Wonka is the name of the man who owns the chocolate factory, remember?" He took the book from Vera, then showed her the cover and read: "'Charlie and the Chocolate Factory: Concerning the adventures of four nasty children and Our Hero with Mr. Willy Wonka and his famous candy plant.'"

"Which word is *hero*?" Vera asked.

"You should know that, too, Vera." Ellis Earl showed her anyway.

"That's what you is," said Vera.

"A *hero*?" Ellis Earl asked, his head tilted to the side.

"'Cause you bring us stuff," Vera answered matter-of-factly. "You bring us books and food. And you show me how to read." She leaned closer to him. "And you told yo' teacher 'bout Jeannette 'n 'em singing. And now they in Memphis, and Mama say they making a record that's gonna be on the radio. And you told that lawyer lady that we need food and they gave us some. And you made us all go to church, and now we moving to a new house." Vera leaned her head against Ellis Earl's arm. "That's how come you a hero."

Ellis Earl hugged her. "Aw, Vera. I ain't no hero. I'm just me, Ellis Earl Brown. I didn't do nothing but speak up like Mr. Foster told me to. And like Uncle Joseph been telling me to, all this time. I just listened to what the grown-ups told me, and I did it."

"And that's what I'm gonna do when I go to school."

"You'll be able to go to the new Head Start center in town next year," Ellis Earl said. "And Beatrice and Deidra can go to school, too, 'cause we can all walk together." Their new house in town was an easy walk to the school. No more relying on Mr. Foster to drive them—or waiting for the county to provide the bus it kept promising was coming. With a smile, he thought about how nice it was that all the children had decided to squeeze in a little tighter to allow Oscar room in Mr. Foster's station wagon. Ellis Earl was happy for his brother to finish out the school year, even if it was for only a few weeks.

He sighed and took in the front room of the house he had lived in for twelve years—the house he had been born in. He would miss this old place, but only because he had shared so many memories here with the people he loved. He was determined to dismiss the bad memories and hold on to the good ones.

The house they were moving to in town was already furnished and had two front rooms. One was called a parlor. Mama said it was the place where company came, so the room always had to stay neat and clean. The new house had a bigger kitchen and a table with enough chairs around it to seat eight people.

The three bedrooms already had beds, but

Mama was still taking the two she had. She would place them in the "other" front room so that Andre, Aaron, and Raymond would have a place to sleep when they came back home after making their record. Jeannette, she said, could sleep in the room with her and Vera.

The new house had three very important things that Ellis Earl never thought he'd see so soon in his life: The new house had a sink in the kitchen. The new house had a toilet indoors. And the new house had electricity.

No more hauling water from the pump. No more emptying the stinky chamber pot or using the outhouse. No more kerosene lamps. And maybe, just maybe, they would be lucky enough to someday own a television like Uncle Joseph.

A short time later, as the family loaded their few belongings on the truck that Uncle Joseph's friend had arrived in, Ellis Earl couldn't help but reflect on the people who had made this possible. The aging widower Deacon Theodore Burton, who had unofficially adopted the Brown family as his own. Since his six children and many grandchildren and great-grandchildren lived out in California and Oregon, he no longer had a need for such a large house. When he said he was giving the deed to Mama, the Brown family thought he meant he was doing a good deed. They had no inkling that giving Mama the deed to the house actually meant she would now own the house, not until Uncle Joseph—who owned a house himself—explained it to them.

Then there was the lady lawyer Miss Marian Wright, who kept her promise and sent another lady to help Mama apply for and receive a monthly allotment of food stamps to help buy food. Not just Mama but also the parents of a few of Ellis Earl's classmates, like Dale and Cassandra. And with Cassandra and her family now being regulars at Emmanuel African Methodist Episcopal Church, Ellis Earl hoped that they, too, would be lucky enough for someone to take them under their wings as Deacon Burton had done with his family.

And of course Ellis Earl knew that he would be forever grateful to Mr. Foster. He had not just been his teacher; to Ellis Earl, he felt like his Willy Wonka.

Ellis Earl recalled the last few pages where Willy Wonka told Mr. Bucket not to worry that the great glass elevator had destroyed his house because he was never going to need it again; Mr. Wonka was moving the entire family to his factory. Mr. Foster wasn't the one giving the Brown family a house, but he was the one who had introduced them to Deacon Burton.

From the yard, Ellis Earl stared at the weather-beaten shack resting atop the large cinder blocks. "It's okay that you rattle when it storms or that you leak when it rains, old house. We thank you for your faithful service all these years. But we won't be needing you anymore. We have a new house now."

The man who had taken Jeannette, Andre, Aaron, and Raymond to Memphis said that they would be receiving something called a contract, and with it would come money. He told them not to expect to get rich overnight, but what they received would be a great help to the family—to the point where Mama would no longer need the food stamps or have to worry about looking for work. Which was a good thing, because there was no one to watch the children while Jeannette was away.

"Come on, Earl!" Carrie Ann yelled from Uncle Joseph's car. "You holding everybody up standing there staring at that old house." She stroked Lucky's back and said, "It's time to go."

Ellis Earl raced to the car and squeezed into the back seat with Oscar, Carrie Ann, and Deidra. Both Beatrice and Vera were wedged between Mama and Uncle Joseph in the front seat.

As he took one last look at the old house, Ellis Earl Brown looked forward to moving not just to a new house, but to a new life.

Author's Note

The idea for this story came to mind as a result of a grocery store visit. While we were in the checkout line, my son noticed the letters *RFK* on a magazine cover and asked me what they meant. I told him who Robert Kennedy was and why he was important enough to headline a magazine. But I didn't think much more about it until a few days later. The *Commercial Appeal* (a newspaper in Memphis, Tennessee) ran several articles on Robert F. Kennedy in 2018, fifty years after his assassination in June 1968. The articles led me to research Kennedy's 1967 visit to the Mississippi Delta during his "Poverty Tour." I had heard about this visit but had never given it much thought until the writer in me realized it was an important part of my own history, much like the Emmett Till connection in my books *Midnight Without a Moon* and *A Sky Full of Stars*.

Reading about Robert Kennedy's visit to Mississippi made me realize it could have easily been my home and my family he visited in April 1967. When Robert Kennedy visited Cleveland, Mississippi, I was just shy of turning ten months old, and my family lived in Rosedale—a small town located eighteen miles west of Cleveland. Nearly everything I read, specifically in the book *Delta Epiphany* by Ellen B. Meacham, about the families Kennedy visited was basically identical to how my family lived. Like with my previous works incorporating the Emmett Till story into my characters' stories, I wanted to give readers a more in-depth look at what life was like for a poor African American family at the time of RFK's visit. I also wanted to show that we were more than the sum of what the media portrayed.

We were more than starving children with distended bellies, raggedy clothing, and dirty faces. We were children who rode to school in station wagons. We were children who received hot meals when we got there. We were children who were encouraged to explore our world through books.

We were children with hopes and dreams.

Yet we were still children who depended on government programs for survival.

Robert Kennedy toured a state whose leaders resented spending money on programs such as Head Start to educate poor Black children. Had it not been for such programs—Head Start, food stamps, Aid to Families with Dependent Children (AFDC) or what's commonly known as welfare, and free school lunches—I don't know whether I would be in a position to write these stories today. However, it is because I grew up dependent upon these social programs that I wanted to give Ellis Earl and his family a more hopeful outcome—one *independent* of these programs and the stigma surrounding them. Hence the success of the fictional singing group, the Brown Blues.

Robert F. Kennedy came to Mississippi to see

for himself whether the poverty problem was as dire as he had heard. I am a living witness that it was. I am also a living witness that, through education and mentoring from caring adults, poverty can be overcome.

A Brief Note Regarding the Original Version of *Charlie and the Chocolate Factory*

During the writing of this book, it came to my attention that in the original 1964 version of *Charlie and the Chocolate Factory*, the Oompa-Loompas were depicted as African pygmies. This depiction of the Oompa-Loompas came across as racist, and the NAACP asked the author, Roald Dahl, to revise the book in 1972. The backstory for the Oompa-Loompas was rewritten with new illustrations as a result. With the setting of *The Lucky Ones* being in 1967, Ellis Earl would have received the original version of *Charlie and the Chocolate Factory*, where the Oompa-Loompas were imports from Africa. I chose not to directly address this in the narrative, and instead decided to allow Ellis Earl, his siblings, and his friend Philip to enjoy Charlie Bucket's story the way so many children have enjoyed it for years—as a wonderful story about a poor boy whose luck changes dramatically when he unwraps a candy bar and finds a golden ticket. A story much like Ellis Earl's.